About the Author

Eleanor Agnes Berry is the author of 21 published books and says her first brush with literature was when she broke windows in Ian Fleming's house at the age of eight. 'He struck me as being a singularly disagreeable man, with no understanding of children,' she recalls. Of Welsh ancestry, she was born and bred in London. She holds a BA Hons degree (a 2:2) in English.

Eleanor specialises in black humour. In many of her books, there is a firm of funeral directors called Crumblebottom and Bongwit. The works of Gorki, Dostoevsky, Gogol, Edgar Allan Poe, James Hadley Chase, George Orwell, Joe Orton and William Harrison-Ainsworth have strongly influenced her writings. While at university she completed an unpublished contextual thesis on the Marquis de Sade (whom she refers to as 'de Soggins'). In her spare time she wrote a grossly indecent book, entitled *The Story of Paddy*, which she had the good sense to burn, and inadvertently set a garage on fire.

After leaving university she worked as a commercial translator, using French and Russian. She then worked as a debt collector a Harley Street specialist, namely the late Dr Victor Ratner, and has since worked intermittently as a medical secretary. She was unfairly sacked from St Bartholomew's Hospital in London because she had been a close friend of the late Robert Maxwell's. (She had worked there for five years!)

Two of her novels are available in Russian and a third, which she refrains from naming, is currently being made into a film. This is her fifteenth book to be published by Book Guild Publishing.

Eleanor is the author of numerous articles in *The Oldie* magazine and has appeared on television and on radio several times, including Radio California. Her interests include Russian literature, Russian folk songs, Irish rebel songs, the cinema, amateur piano playing, sensational court cases, the medical profession, entertaining her nephews, to whom she is extremely close, and swimming across Marseille harbour for kicks. When she dies, she will have her ashes scattered over Marseille harbour, her favourite place.

Eleanor Berry is the maternal niece of the late, famous, self-confessed gypsy author, Eleanor Smith, after whom she was named. Sadly, Eleanor Smith died before Eleanor Berry was born.

Books by Eleanor Berry

The Story of Paddy (A pornographic book – not published)
Tell Us a Sick One Jakey (A black comedy about a mortuary attendant who dies of a brain tumour. Out of print.)
Never Alone with Rex Malone (A black comedy about Robert Maxwell's relationship with a crooked funeral director.)
Someone's Been Done Up Harley
O, Hitman, My Hitman!
The Most Singular Adventures of Eddy Vernon
Take It Away, It's Red!
Stop the Car, Mr Becket! (Formerly *The Rendon Boy to the Grave Is Gone.*)
Robert Maxwell as I Knew Him (out of print – blast it!)
Cap'n Bob and Me
McArandy was Hanged on the Gibbet High
The House of the Weird Doctors
Sixty Funny Stories
The Most Singular Adventures of Sarah Lloyd
Alandra Varinia – Sarah's Daughter
The Rise and Fall of Mad Silver Jaxton
By the Fat of Unborn Leopards
The Killing of Lucinda Maloney
My Old Pal was a Junkie (Available in Russian.)
Your Father Had to Swing, You Little Bastard! (Available in Russian.)
An Eye for a Tooth and a Limb for an Eye
Help me, Help me, It's Red!
Come Sweet Sexton, Tend my Grave

Reviews

Tell Us a Sick One Jakey
'This book is quite repulsive!' Sir Michael Havers, Attorney General

Never Alone with Rex Malone
'A ribald, ambitious black comedy, a story powerfully told.' Stewart Steven, *The Daily Mail*

'I was absolutely flabbergasted when I read it!' *Robert Maxwell*

Robert Maxwell as I Knew Him
'One of the most amusing books I have read for a long time. Eleanor Berry is an original.' Elisa Segrave, *The Literary Review*

'Undoubtedly the most amusing book I have read all year.' Julia Llewellyn-Smith, *The Times*

'With respect and I repeat, with very great respect, because I know you're a lady, but all you ever do is just go on and on and on and on about this bleeding bloke.' *Reggie Kray.*

Cap'n Bob and Me
'A comic masterpiece.' *The Times*

'As befits the maternal granddaughter of F.E. Smith (famous barrister who never lost a case) Eleanor Berry has a sharp tone of phrase and a latent desire for upsetting people. Campaigning for her hero, Robert Maxwell, in a General Election, she climbed to the top of the Buckingham Town Hall with intent to erect the red flag. Eleanor Berry fits into the long tradition of British eccentricity.' Stewart Graham, *The Spectator*

Someone's Been Done Up Harley
'In this book, Eleanor Berry's dazzling wit hits the Harley Street scene. Her extraordinary humour had me in stitches.'
Thelma Masters, *The Oxford Times*

O, Hitman, My Hitman!
'Eleanor Berry's volatile pen is at it again. This time, she takes her readers back to the humorously eccentric Harley Street community. She also introduces Romany gypsies and travelling circuses, a trait which she has inherited from her self-confessed maternal gypsy aunt, the late writer, Eleanor Smith, after whom she was named. Like Smith, Berry is an inimitable and delightfully natural writer.' Kev Zein, *The Johannesburg Evening Sketch*

McArandy was Hanged on the Gibbet High
'We have here a potboiling, swashbuckling blockbuster, which is rich in adventure, intrigue, history, amorous episodes and black humour. The story Eleanor Berry tells is multi-coloured, multi-faceted and nothing short of fantastic.' Angel Z. Hogan, *The Daily Melbourne Times*

The Most Singular Adventures of Eddy Vernon
'Rather a hot book for bedtime.' the late Nigel Dempster, *The Daily Mail*

Stop the Car, Mr Becket! (formerly The Rendon Boy to the Grave is Gone)
'This book makes for fascinating reading, as strange, black humoured and entertaining as Eleanor Berry's other books which came out before it.' It is to be noted that Eleanor is deeply embarrassed by this book. *Gaynor Evans, Bristol Evening Post*

Sixty Funny Stories
'This book is a laugh a line.' Elisa Segrave, writer and diarist.

The House of the Weird Doctors
'This delightful medical caper puts even A.J. Cronin in the shade.' Noel I. Leskin, *The Stethoscope*

The Most Singular Adventures of Sarah Lloyd
'A riotous read from start to finish.' Ned McMurphy, *The Irish Times*

Alandra Varinia – Sarah's Daughter
'Eleanor Berry manages to maintain her raw and haunting wit as much as ever.' Dwight C. Farr, *The Texas Chronicle*

The Rise and Fall of Mad Silver Jaxton
'This time, Eleanor Berry tries her versatile hand at politics. Her sparkling wit and the reader's desire to turn the page are still in evidence. Eleanor Berry is unique.' Don F. Saunderson, *The South London Review*

'This is a dark, disturbing but at the same time hilarious tale of a megalomaniac dictator by the always readable and naughty Eleanor Berry.' The late Sally Farmiloe, award-winning actress and author.

By the Fat of Unborn Leopards
'Could this ribald, grisly-humoured story about a right-wing British newspaper magnate's daughter, possibly be autobiographical, by any chance?' Peggy-Lou Kadinsky, *The Washington Globe*

'Fantastically black. A scream from beginning to end.'
Charles Kidd, Editor of *Debrett's Peerage*

The Killing of Lucinda Maloney
'This is the funniest book I've read for months,' Samantha Morris, *The Exeter Daily News*

My Old Pal was a Junkie
'Eleanor Berry is to literature what Hieronymus Bosch is to art. As with all Miss Berry's books, the reader has a burning urge to turn the page.' Sonia Drew, *The International Continental Review*

Your Father Had to Swing, You Little Bastard!
'A unique display of black humour which somehow fails to depress the reader.' Craig McLittle, *The Rugby Gazette*

'This book is an unheard of example of English black humour. Eleanor Berry is almost a reincarnation of our own beloved Dostoevsky.' Sergei Robkov, Russian magazine, *Minuta*

An Eye for a Tooth and a Limb for an Eye – A Story of Revenge
'Words are Eleanor Berry's toys and her use of them is boundless.' Mary Hickman, professional historian and writer.

Help Me, Help Me, It's Red!
'Despite the sometimes weighty portent of this book, a sense of subtle, dry and powerfully engaging humour reigns throughout its pages. The unexpected twist is stupendous.'
Stephen Carson, *The Carolina Sun*

'This is grim humour at its very best. The most challenging and most delightful novel I have read in six months.' Scott Mason-Jones, *The New York Globe*

Come Sweet Sexton, Tend my Grave
'This is a grisly but highly amusing and entertaining book. I couldn't put it down from beginning to end.'
Jason John Goldberg, *Time Magazine*

Come Sweet Sexton, Tend My Grave

Eleanor Berry

www.eleanorberry.net

The Book Guild Ltd

First published in Great Britain in 2017 by
The Book Guild Ltd
9 Priory Business Park
Wistow Road, Kibworth
Leicestershire, LE8 0RX
Freephone: 0800 999 2982
www.bookguild.co.uk
Email: info@bookguild.co.uk
Twitter: @bookguild

Typeset in Baskerville

Printed and bound in Great Britain by CPI Group (UK) Ltd, Croydon, CR0 4YY

ISBN 978 1911320 265

British Library Cataloguing in Publication Data.
A catalogue record for this book is available from the British Library

In memory of my beloved brother, Nicky.

The Mission of Professor Stone

Professor Isaac Stone was thirty-five years old. His home town was Boston and his place of work was London. Although he was a Professor in severe mental disorders, he had a short temper and a tongue like an adder. He was savagely intolerant of unfortunates who did not share his tastes, interests and opinions.

He was good-looking and he knew it. He was five foot ten inches tall, had thick black hair and piercing grey eyes.

His subject was reactive, catatonic schizophrenia.

Strangely, he had a steady girlfriend to whom he was devoted. Her name was Anna Jacobson. She was thirty years old. She, too, was in the medical profession. Like the Professor, she was from Boston. She had a calming effect on him whenever he became bad-tempered.

Unlike that of other members of his profession, his life style was extravagant and his tastes were expensive. He worked hard and played hard. He was just as devoted to his career as he was to his decadent pursuits, once his days' duties were finished.

He was a *gourmet* and was almost over-zealous about his wines and the food he ate with them. He considered it beneath his dignity to enter a hotel or a restaurant with fewer than five stars. He loved speedboats and gambling as much as he loved the opera, the theatre and the cinema. Whenever he gambled, he was a poor loser. Also, he was incapable of laughing at jokes made at his expense.

It was a bitterly cold January day in London and it was snowing heavily. The Professor was inappropriately but smartly dressed. He was wearing a navy blue cashmere sweater, a white open-necked shirt and recently ironed navy blue trousers.

He also had on a thick Austrian hunting coat which helped, to some extent, to keep out the cold.

Just as he arrived at the Rudyard Kipling Hospital for Mental Disorders, he leapt out of his chauffeur-driven Bentley and jumped up and down on the spot.

"Are you cold, Professor?" asked his chauffeur inanely.

The Professor clapped his fur-lined gloves together.

"Looks like it, doesn't it?" he snapped and rushed into the building.

He walked towards the desk in the centre of a huge high-ceilinged room, its walls lined with plastered caryatids. He was reminded of the sort of room that Mussolini would have received his ministers in.

The receptionist at the desk liked the look of him and smiled. Her name was on her lapel; It was Louise Spencer. He failed to return her smile. She was slim and had short peroxide hair, parted at the side and a maroon woollen mini-dress.

The Professor's features, combined with his elegant clothes, contrasted with the looks of the many shabby-looking doctors, who came to her desk every day. He produced a card which Louise accepted.

"I've come here to interview a seriously ill patient called Esmerelda Harris. Her hospital number is 100623," he began tersely. "Her room number is 1006 and she is on the fourteenth floor." The Professor spoke with a trace of a Boston accent. He produced another card with more stamps on it than the first one. Louise smiled again and accepted the second card as well. Once more, he failed to return her smile.

She handed the two cards to a blue-shirted porter with a series of keys on his belt. On seeing the keys, the Professor angrily raised his eyes to the ceiling as he despised bureaucracy.

"My subject is reactive catatonic schizophrenia," he explained to Louise with a rasp in his voice. He added, "I have to complete a two-hundred thousand word thesis on the subject, citing an outstanding case as my main theme," repeated the Professor. "I have given the details to Miss Spencer and she has fed them into the computer."

The Professor took particular pleasure in repeating himself because he liked to give the impression that he considered other people to be half witted., "My patient, Esmerelda Harris, suffers from reactive catatonic schizophrenia." He was in a particularly bad mood that day, because he had played badly at the casino in the Ritz the night before.

"Oh, that one?" one of the blue-shirted porters said. He spoke with a thick cockney accent. "That's a vegetable for you if ever there was one. The 'ole 'ospital knows what 'appened to Esmerelda Harris. She went somewhere where she knew she wasn't supposed to go to and she saw something there that drove 'er barmy.

"Where the hell did she go?" asked the Professor irritably.

The porter ignored his question. He spoke with a thick cockney accent. "Er friend, – Annabella someone, dunno the surname. She saw whatever it was, went 'ome and 'anged 'erself. They didn't find 'er body till after three weeks."

The porter was unmoved by the look of frustration on the Professor's face, and the Professor listened with disgust to what he had to say.

The porter continued, "They 'ave to pump stuff into Miss 'Arris, just to get 'er to talk to 'er shrinks. When the stuff wears off, I wouldn't like to watch her withdrawal symptoms for all the rice in China. 'Ere, I'll take the Professor up to the fourteenth floor. 'Old the fort, will you?" he said to yet another blue-shirted porter, who was sitting in the hall with his feet up, doing the *Sun* crossword.

"It's such a fuckin' shame," said the first porter. "Miss 'Arris's got a room to 'erself with a beautiful view of London, and she's too ill to get out of bed and fling 'erself out of the bleedin' winda."

"There's no need for foul language," said the Professor, his voice raised.

The porter called for a lift. He and the Professor got in. The two men eventually reached the fourteenth floor.

The porter showed the Professor to the office of Sister McNabe, who was responsible for seeing that Esmerelda did not commit suicide.

"Some of the patients 'ere give you the creeps, but I think this young woman's quite 'armless," the porter said. These were probably the kindest words that a man of his ghoulish disposition had ever uttered in his life.

Sister McNabe looked butch and had a thick Scottish accent. The Professor suspected that she had lesbian tendencies. She had more keys on her belt than a warden at the Lubyanka.[1*]

"Just wait a wee moment. I'll take you along," said Sister McNabe to the Professor. She tried one key after the other until she found the right one.

"You're only allowed in here for two wee hours a day," said Sister McNabe to the Professor, adding, "The drug that Esmerelda has to take to get her to speak and remember things with the minimum amount of psychological pain, wears off after two hours.

Esmerelda's room was small. Because of the splendid view from the window, showing the snow-covered dome of St Paul's Cathedral, the Professor envied its occupant. The walls of the room were white and uncovered except for a fake Picasso. Heat came through the pale blue linoleum floor. Near the window was a large table and in one corner of the room was an almost empty

1 The Lubyanka: A notorious, unheated prison in Moscow in Stalin's Russia where prisoners were tortured.

wardrobe. In another corner was a wash-basin with a glass shelf above it, on which was a tube of Colgate Total toothpaste, a bottle of Listerine mouthwash, a face flannel, a cake of Pears soap and a bottle of unused toilet water. There was also some face powder, some mascara and some eye-liner on the shelf.

Esmerelda was in her early twenties. She was wearing a black cotton night-gown which she had pulled up to her waist to keep out the heat coming from the floor.

Round her head and shoulders was a long mane of curly reddish blonde hair. Her face was lit by a pair of huge, violet blue eyes that were out of focus and which stared inwards at each other.

Although there was something eerie about Esmerelda's eyes, the Professor felt sick to the stomach with lust – an emotion which he had only experienced once before in his life. This was when he had first seen his wife at a distance across a room before being introduced to her. On their wedding night, he found her dead on the floor of their matrimonial bedroom. She had slashed her wrists. This was because she had suddenly suspected that her marriage would be a failure. She had realized that the Professor was foul-mouthed, bad-tempered and that he did not suffer fools gladly.

The Professor looked greedily at Esmerelda. He averted his eyes abruptly from the steely stare of Sister McNabe who was standing in front of him. He desperately tried to hide the lust which the patient's beauty had aroused in him by getting out his typewriter and starting to type, 'THE QUICK BROWN FOX JUMPED OVER THE LAZY DOG, just for the sake of having something to do with his trembling hands.

"If you think you're going to bring a wee typewriter in here, you can forget it," said the Sister unpleasantly to the Professor, who had more letters after his name than she had imitation pearls round her neck. "Esmerelda isn't strong enough to put up with a noise like that." Suddenly, she noticed his physical condition caused by the lust which he could not conceal. "We can't have everything we want in life, can we, Professor," she said vulgarly. She phoned Reception and asked for a word processor.

Two blue-shirted porters came into Esmerelda's room with a trolley carrying a word processor. The Professor was bitter and had always loathed men wearing blue shirts. This was due to an experience which he had had when he was six years old: a motorbike rider, wearing a blue shirt, had run over and killed his dog. "You should have had the bastard on a lead!" the motorbike rider had said, and rode off into the distance, leaving the boy by the side of the road, weeping

"Why the hell do there have to be two of you pushing one trolley?" the Professor shouted at the two porters.

"Union rules is bleedin' union rules," one of the porters replied. On noticing the Professor's physical condition and the way in which he was staring at Esmerelda, he cackled coarsely, "Blimey guv, you'll be bloomin' lucky!"

"Don't be so damned impertinent," shouted the Professor. He refrained from giving the porter a left hook.

For the first time since they had met, Sister McNabe spoke sympathetically to the Professor. Somehow, she felt allied to him because of her dislike of union representatives.

"There's just one thing I thought I ought to warn you about," she said, "Esmerelda can be quite an arrogant young lass, when she's not what they call 'catatonic'."

'A dame as pretty as that has every reason to be arrogant,' shouted the Professor, adding, "I'm astounded to hear you referring to this matter!"

Sister McNabe felt snubbed. "There's nothing to be worried about. You'll only have to be with the wee lass for two hours a day, weekdays only". The Sister added, "Her speech will sometimes appear to be deliberate, monotonous and unvaried in delivery." As she continued to speak, the Sister's Scottish accent became more and more pronounced. She added, "The poor wee lass can be quite humorous in a dour, black-humoured sort of way. She only lasts for about two hours, as I said earlier. As soon as her left eye begins to twitch, just ring the wee bell, and I'll get the orderlies out to hold her down, while I give her her injection."

"What the hell do you mean by the 'orderlies'?" asked the Professor aggressively.

"I meant the porters. They all wear blue shirts as you probably noticed."

"Lord save us! Can't you give her another drug? What you are giving her sounds very inhuman," snapped the Professor. "This time I want an intelligent answer from you."

The Sister replied in a dead pan tone of voice as if she were announcing that a train was going to stop at Reading. "She only lasts for about two wee hours, as I said. Besides, you want her to talk, don't you? Only after her wee story is down on paper, can she undergo proper psychoanalysis. Once we've got her story down from beginning to end, we'll be able to wean her off the drugs and treat her."

"What drugs are you giving her, for Christ's sake?" shouted the Professor. "This time I'll tolerate no nonsense and longwindedness either!"

"That is of no concern to an academic," replied Sister McNabe tersely. She added, "Your job is to get out of Esmerelda what an ordinary psychiatrist can't. Once we find out where she went, why she went there, what she saw there, and why what she saw drove her mad, then and only then can we hope to control her symptoms."

"Christ!" shouted the Professor. "Why the hell can't you just say to her, 'Where did you go?' You are wasting my time, Sister. I'm a busy man. Besides, you're talking in riddles. You come over as being amazingly stupid."

Sister McNabe burst into tears. She left the Professor in room 1006, with a word processor, a printer and a woman who reminded him of Lucrezia Borgia.

THE PATIENT SPEAKS

"The injection has taken effect. The drugs have reached my brain. I will talk now," Esmerelda began. Her speech was indeed monotonous and deliberate as Sister McNabe had stated. She had a trace of an upper class accent. She continued, "All this business is about a certain Charlie Yates. I was a close friend of his. He is dead now. In fact, if you are typing everything I say, I would like you to entitle my story, *'Come Sweet Sexton, Tend My Grave'."* Esmerelda continued,

"My closest friends live in London where I have lived all my life. I used to spend most evenings with them, in restaurants and pubs mainly, sometimes in private houses and flats.

"If you want to know what my interests are, they are many and varied. Among them are Russian folk songs, entertaining my nephews, to whom I am extremely close and swimming backwards and forwards across Marseille harbour for kicks. When I die, I shall have my ashes scattered over Marseille harbour which is my favourite place."

Esmerelda changed the subject abruptly. "Incidentally, I thought I'd mention this in passing, nothing pleases me more than the sight of a slightly overweight man who wears his tie loosened at the neck. You may well ask me what this has got to do with my friend, Charlie Yates."

"Did he wear his tie loosened at the neck?" asked the Professor.

"No, he did not," replied Esmerelda assertively. "He never wore a tie." She continued, changing the subject once more, "The barrier between the horrible and the beautiful is thick to some. To me, it is thinner than a thread of cotton.

"The sight of a sixty-year old man's body, with its sinews stretched to drain his face of the ravages of suffering and the indignity of age, is beautiful after death.

"It becomes a greater work of art than that which can be found in any gallery. The touch of his face, as smooth and as cool as marble in its very silence, speaks louder than any symphony. Its cream-like serenity, arousing desire because of its vulnerable sacredness, nurtures the soul more deeply than any peace.

"I don't want to go on about this subject for longer than I need, and I'll finish off with a quotation from the works of Edgar Allan Poe who is a hero of mine: He is not referred to as 'the Divine Edgar' for nothing. The following words appear in one of his essays, entitled *The Philosophy of Composition*.

> *"'Of all melancholy topics, what, according to the universal understanding of mankind, is the most beautiful? Death is the obvious reply.*
> *"'And when is the most melancholy of topics the most poetical?…'*
> *The answer is obvious – when it allies itself to beauty.'"*

"Death and beauty lie side by side and sexual desire is conceived of their union. Like all marriages, they sometimes come into conflict. However there is a division between what concerns you personally and what does not, and he who has loved a dead person, cannot gloat over what he sees. The conflict between the voyeur and the feeler is not an easy conflict to bear. He who tries to be both, ends up in an institution like this."

The Professor sighed and adjusted his tie.

There was another pause broken by Esmerelda.

"I enjoy being dishonest," she said suddenly. "My uncle

once gave me a watch worth £150 for my birthday. I rang up an insurance company and reported it as having been stolen. The insurance company gave me £250. That's what I said the watch was worth.

"Two weeks later, I took the watch to Marseille where I flogged it for the equivalent of £500.

"A more honest way of earning your living is whipping masochists but that's pretty hard work, and strenuous too. You can get £800 a night out of a wealthy masochist, particularly if he's an Arab, and because he pays you in cash, you can claim dole money as well. So although I'm not as fancy a gangster as my dear old friend, the late Reggie Kray, I can count myself as a damned good gangster in my own right!"

"Who the hell was Reggie Kray? He sounds like a character out of a *Rupert Bear* book to me," said the Professor impatiently.

"Don't you know who Reggie Kray was? He and his twin brother, Ronnie Kray, were gang leaders. They were sent down by a fierce judge called Melford Stevenson in 1969. They were given thirty years each."

"I suppose you condone violence?" said the Professor in a disagreeable tone of voice.

"Sure thing man!" said Esmerelda imitating his accent. She added "Long before they brought me here, I also earned my living by translating commercial letters into French and Russian. Those are my best languages, apart from English, of course. I once interpreted an argument between a Frenchman and a Russian about a complex medical matter and I couldn't stop shouting. Nerves it was. No more. In the end I was bunged out. Besides, I can only speak Marseillaise fishwives' French and Russian with a thick Siberian accent. As for German, the only German I know is "*Churchill ist ein Arschloch*" which Hitler used to say from time to time. The vulgar remark is self-explanatory.

"I am also a pretty good medical secretary. I have worked in almost every national health hospital in London. Like my late friend Charlie Yates, I enjoy dining out about my experiences. The pattern of medical secretarial work is roughly the same. At four thirty, after we have finished our work, in comes someone with a tray of poor quality tea. The other secretaries slurp their tea and wipe their mouths on their sleeves, which revolts me.

"I don't care for this ritual, to say the least. I bring in a bottle of ginger beer (one of my favourite non-alcoholic drinks). I drink it alone, not in front of all these other people. The office usually stinks of tea, and cigarettes, which make me retch.

"As I said, my friends have never stopped asking me questions about the medical secretarial work I do and my work as a typist of post-mortem reports. This is a subject, about which I like to occupy the limelight. Oh, how I love to be the centre of attention!

"Damned show-off!" muttered the Professor. "Go on."

"One evening, I saw a stranger sitting in the pub with my friends. He was between about twenty and twenty-five years old.

"He had a very pretty, faunlike face and mischievous hazel eyes. He listened to me attentively. His mood fluctuated between low spirits and high spirits. I couldn't make him out. A good friend of mine called Stanley Trout, introduced me to the newcomer. His name was Charlie Yates and he was a mature student doing a course at London University. Trout introduced Charlie to me and added that he was known as the "court jester". He described Charlie as being a "pure treasure".

"What's wrong, Charlie? You're very quiet today," said a man I hardly knew.

"I've just got back from this hospital," said Charlie. He spoke with a slight lisp. He looked distressed and amused at the same time.

"I had an old school friend called Douglas Cuthead," Charlie told his listeners. He slumped over the table and collapsed in paroxysms of nervous giggles, combined with tears. Trout knew Charlie well enough to realize that his friend was both amused and broken-hearted at the same time. It later transpired that Cuthead had been as close to Charlie as a brother and that he had died just before Charlie came to the pub. He came to the pub because he didn't want to let his friends down.'"

"The next evening we all went to a *pizzeria*. Charlie was there and I told him that I was really sorry about Douglas Cuthead. Later, we became friends.

"That evening was 16th April. It was Charlie's birthday, and although he was still depressed because of Cuthead's death, he was able to tell black-humoured jokes. A Spanish aunt of his had given him some castanets. He showed a keen sense of musicianship by singing a song to the tune of the *Habenera* aria from *Carmen*:

"I'll tell you the tragedy of a woman called Joan.
It was through the noose she came into her own.
This poor unfortunate could not cope,
So she hanged herself on a yard of rope."

The song continued and became increasingly black-humoured.

"Suddenly, Charlie stopped singing. Trout more sensed what was wrong with him, took him by the hand and led him outside into the street. Charlie agreed to go to another the pub which we often frequented called the *Monkey's Paw* in Chelsea. Trout and Charlie travelled in Trout's Volkswagen Polo (his second car).

"We all followed them. My best friend, Annabella Sikes was with us. I got into Annabella's bright red Ford Escort. Annabella had had more to drink than I had, so I took the wheel.

"Unfortunately, there was someone else with us. He sat in the back seat. He was a dreadful fellow called Sam Sutton and he called himself a writer. He could not stop talking in a schoolmistressy way about the necessity of wearing seat belts. The following night, Sam recited an utterly disgusting poem entitled

Seat Belts. The author's publisher has refrained from printing the poem.

Charlie then described Douglas Cuthead's condition. "Tell us about Douglas Cuthead's death, then, Charlie," said Sam who was universally disliked. We were all sitting in a restaurant after hearing Sam's revolting poem. Charlie cracked a repulsive joke and graphically described Cuthead's gory condition and the reactions of the luckless people on his ward.

Charlie's audience forced themselves to laugh. Trout was the only person who knew that Charlie's hysterical giggling was a substitute for tears.

"There were three other men on Cuthead's ward, apart from Cuthead himself," said Charlie, his lisp more pronounced. "One was fat Steve who weighed thirty stone and who defecated on the floor almost every night. He rolled out of bed like a beach ball and made continuous wind-breaking noises.

"Another man was Sweating Joe who couldn't stop grunting. Every afternoon, he had diarrheoa and wiped his bottom with the front page of the *Daily Mail*.

"Added to these patients was Dying George and last of all, Douglas Cuthead. His condition and subsequent death was the most repellant of all…"

"I didn't care for the full story of Douglas Cuthead's gory death and I didn't realize at the time that Charlie's narrative was an attempt to hide his grief.

"This is not a laughing matter," I said sternly.

"You're a fine one to talk!" barked the Professor.

"Show me your hand," said Charlie. "I can tell fortunes as well as unpleasant stories." I pushed my right hand palm upwards under his eyes.

"What can you see, you horrible man?" I asked. There was a pause in which I detected an aura of eeriness and a premonition that something very nasty was going to happen to me one day in the not too distant future.

"Ha, ha!" said Charlie. "Your life will one day be saved by my brain!"

"In that case, you'd better sharpen your wits!" I said in a hostile tone of voice.

Trout was furious. There are very few occasions when I have known him to be angry. He screws up his face like a rat and makes a strange, hissing noise. On the first occasion, a left wing porter threw all his *Vuitton* suitcases onto the tracks at Victoria Station. Trout gave him a left hook. On the second occasion, he got very drunk and drove his Bentley (his other smarter car) from London to Birmingham for reasons best known to himself. He was confronted by two policemen as he was driving the wrong way down a one way street. The first policeman did all the talking:

"Excuse me, sir, I'd like a word with you about your driving."

"I'm not familiar with these parts. I was just sauntering down from London for a snappy fuckette."

"Have you been drinking?"

"Certainly not!"

"Breathe into this, will you, please."

"Trout was way over the alcoholic limit.

"Cuff him, Ned," the policeman said to his colleague. "I'm slinging you down the nick."

"I won't be treated like this!" shouted Trout. "Who are you anyway? You're just a bureaucratic ratbag of a policeman. Also, I'll have you know that I keep a photograph of Sir Winston Churchill on my bedside table." Trout was banned from driving for a year.

"He was furious with me on the third occasion. He told me, with his voice raised, that I had grossly misunderstood Charlie and that I had no business insulting him.

One of Charlie's Stories

A Most Singular Encounter between Herr Grübler and Signor Dementia

Herr Grübler, a German, and Signor Dementia, an Italian, lived in adjacent apartments on the tenth floor of a high-rise block in West Berlin. I heard this story from Luigi Dementia who is Signor Dementia's son. Signor Dementia was tall, slim and prosperous. He had dark hair, green eyes and was forty years old. He was happily married but his wife was away. One could describe him as being happy with his lot in life.

"Herr Grübler, on the other hand, was a sad, fifty-year-old man with grey hair and pale blue, Aryan eyes which were alarmingly piercing. He was stocky-looking and red-faced, due to his heavy alcohol consumption. He always left his front door ajar from ten o'clock in the evening onwards, so that his boyfriends could visit him.

"Apart from the odd boyfriend he had an illegitimate daughter.

"Herr Grübler was not a social acquaintance of Signor Dementia and when they were not using the lift, the two men never met. Each knew what the other looked like but they had never spoken to each other until this particular occasion.

"Herr Grübler had a lot of worries. He had once been a successful publisher but his firm had gone bust. He jogged and went for long walks every day to ease his disappointment.

His readers had turned a lot of his authors' manuscripts down. He was inundated by poison pen letters from the authors whom his firm had rejected. Some of these letters contained threats of violence. Somehow, the rejected authors had found out his address.

The writer of one of the poison pen letters even threatened to throw sulphuric acid into the face of his illegitimate daughter who lived with her mother.

"He began to walk in his sleep. Sometimes, he woke up leaning over his balcony rail outside his apartment. There were times when he woke up wishing that he had leaned too far over his balcony rail and had fallen on to the dual carriageway below.

This time, when he was walking in his sleep, he did not walk onto his balcony. For some reason had put on a pair of striped hiking socks, lace-up boots with studded soles and a wide-brimmed straw hat. Apart from these bizarre clothes, he was naked. Signor Dementia had temporarily left his front door open in order to put his rubbish down the chute. Herr Grübler walked into Signor Dementia's apartment and was woken by a hand on his shoulder. Since Signor Dementia spoke no German, and Herr Grübler spoke no Italian, the conversation between the two men took place in English which they both spoke fluently.

"What the devil do you think you are doing in my apartment, dressed in that manner?" shouted Signor Dementia.

"I live in this apartment," the astounded Herr Grübler eventually managed to splutter.

"You lie! you lie! you lie! you lie!," bellowed the Italian, adding, "Next time you visit my apartment, kindly wait for an invitation."

Herr Grübler looked round the hallway into which he had wandered, and concluded that the interior decoration was different to that in his own apartment.

"Not very good tastes in interior decoration," he said defensively. However, his strangely clad legs weakened and he fainted.

When he came round, Signor Dementia was holding him by the wrists. Herr Grübler sprang to his feet.

"It seems that you do not realize how very dangerous it is to wake someone up when they are walking in their sleep," he stated, with a clipped Germanic rasp, "Your action might have caused me to go into cardiac failure."

The Italian looked at the German.

The German continued to stare at the Italian. Eventually, he spoke.

"Do not ever again wake someone up when they are walking in their sleep," Herr Grübler continued. He was outwardly unaffected by the idiot that he had made of himself. He added, "I don't go to Italy and wake Italians up when they are sleep-walking, so kindly don't come here and wake me up when I am sleep-walking!"

"Signor Dementia waved his arms in the air, like a swimmer calling for help. "But you *walked* into my apartment," he said, helplessly.

"Maybe I did and I fainted. When I was unconscious, how did you know that I was not in cardiac failure? Did you check to see if mein heart und mein lungs vere vorking?" shouted Herr Grübler.

"Why are you shouting?" asked Signor Dementia mildly. His speech was clipped like the speech of someone speaking to a raving lunatic.

Herr Grübler marched towards the front door of the Italian's apartment. As he left the premises, he found that he had left his wide-brimmed straw hat behind. He realized that the hat was essential to hide his nakedness in the corridor, but he could not bring himself to ask the dumbfounded Signor Dementia to give it to him.

"Everyone liked Charlie's story," said Esmerelda proudly.

The Professor turned towards her. I find this story very sad," he said with a sneer. "In fact, I find it pathetic."

Another of Charlie's stories

Stiffs Part One

We were all in the *Monkey's* Paw once more. Charlie was speaking in a loud, resonant manner and his lisp was more marked than usual.

The first time I entered a mortuary (that is before I worked in one), I went in out of morbid curiosity. My agency sent me to answer the phones in the cardiac department of the London Hospital. I went to the mortuary during my tea-break.

I put on a white coat to make my appearance look authentic, carried a buff-coloured file under my arm to make it look like a patient's file and asked a porter in an authoritative way where the mortuary was. The porter directed me.

I went down a corridor and through a door which had the words 'STRICTLY NO ADMITTANCE' on top of it. I took a chance and went straight in. The place was dimly lit and there was no-one about.

I opened a drawer and saw a dead body lying under a sheet. I wanted to see if it had belonged to a man or a woman. It was a man's body.

Suddenly, a man wearing a plastic coat and rubber boots came up to me. He was tall, had bright red hair and a long pointed nose.

Who the hell are you and what do you think you're doing here?" shrieked the man who was about forty years old and whose face I shall remember to this day. "This is a dead body that I've got here," he added.

"I can see that, can't I, mate," I replied.

Trout laughed. His laughter sounded like an old-fashioned typewriter carriage return.

"What did you say to the man?" he asked.

"I said the first thing that came into my head: I said, "That's the first stiff I've seen since Lenin. Have you ever been to Moscow?"

"No, I have not been to Moscow!" shouted the incensed mortician, "and I don't have the slightest intention of going anywhere near the place. I hope I won't be obliged to make myself clearer than this to get you to fuck off!"

"There's no need to be so bad-tempered," I said, adding, "People who work in mortuaries usually think that they *own* the dead."

I went away ignoring the man's echoing calls of "who are you?" which became fainter and fainter, as I put as much distance between him and myself as I possibly could."

"That's not funny, either. That's pathetic too, like the last story you told," said the Professor. Esmerelda snarled at him.

Stiffs, Part Two[2*]

I had better luck working at Bede's Hospital. Bede's is the oldest hospital in London. It was founded during the reign of King Henry the First by a friar who received a vision from a saint, telling him to build the foundations of a hospital for the poor of London. The hospital is close to West Smithfield and is within

2 [*]Bede's Hospital is modelled on St Bartholomew's Hospital (Barts), which the author was sacked from, because she had been a close friend of the late Robert Maxwell's. She had worked there for five years! The doctor responsible for her sacking, was called Dr. LARRY Baker. He was profoundly jealous of her friendship with Mr Maxwell.

walking distance from the Old Bailey. The oldest parts of the hospital, like the hospital chapel, are still intact.

To get to Bede's, you have to go through West Smithfield. You then walk through a courtyard with a garden and a fountain in the centre. The hospital has imposing walls of blackening grey. In the summer, medical students continuously throw each other into the water.

I was told to work in the post-mortem room. One of the managers invited me to let him buy me a drink after work. He was a dwarf and he had a thick Welsh accent. His name was Leslie Evans. He asked my agency for a temporary porter. He must have taken a fancy to me, because he asked my agency to send me back to Bede's repeatedly. I had to work on the first floor of the Chaffinch Stream Block. Post-mortems take place on Tuesday mornings when medical students are expected to attend. I was fascinated by the post-mortems.

Evans was three foot, four inches tall. He asked me for my name. Very foolishly, I gave it to him. He asked me for my phone number as well. When I wasn't thinking, I gave him that too.

Even when I wasn't working at Bede's, he rang me up at six-thirty every morning and suggested that we meet for lunch. I refused his invitation and said that I was studying. As is almost always the case with people connected with the dead, he was a pathological hypochondriac.

The worst is still to come. I had a ghastly hangover, and had not got to sleep until four o'clock in the morning. At six thirty that same morning, my phone rang again. It was Leslie Evans.

"Look, Charlie," he said, "I want to talk to you man to man. I've got something desperately important to tell you… Will you wish me luck?"

"Who's the lucky lady? Isn't six thirty in the morning rather an unsuitable time of day to propose to her?"

"You don't understand," said Evans. "It's something a lot more sinister."

"Sinister?"

"Yes. I'm standing in the hall in my dressing-gown and slippers and I'm drinking a cup of tea."

"How absolutely riveting! What are you going to do when you've finished your tea? Are you going to make another cup?"

"No, I'm going to take a very deep breath," said Evans ponderously. Suddenly, as if he were about to jump out of a plane, he said with a terrifying sense of urgency, "I'm going to do a spit!"

"How thrilling!" I replied, baffled, "Who are you going to spit at? Anyone I know?"

"It's not that kind of spit," Evans explained patiently, adding, "it's a carcinoma spit."

"I wouldn't know what a carcinoma spit was, if I saw one walking down the street. It sounds like some dreadful American ice cream mix to me," I answered as politely as possible. "What do you mean?" I added.

"You see, Charlie," Evans said hoarsely, "Carcinoma means cancer in layman's terms."

"Cancer?"

"Yes, and I want to make quite sure I haven't got it. Cancer of the throat, that is."

"Surely there's no reason why you should have it, is there?"

"You must understand that none of us are getting any younger. I've got this old handkerchief that my father used to own. In fact, it's on the hall table, next to my cup of tea. There's a nice lot of brown gunk in my handkerchief now. I'll do another spit shortly. The stuff comes up like a yoyo after a cup of tea. I'm going to pluck up the courage and have a jolly good old spit, once more!" Evans made a revolting hoiking noise. "Did you hear that, Charlie?" he asked.

"Jolly good, sir!" I said, half asleep and half awake. I heard a voice saying: "I've done the spit, and I'm going to wham it under the microscope by my bed, now."

"Have you really got a microscope by your bed?" I asked.

"Yes, of course, I've got one by my bed, so if I go down with carcinoma, I'll be the first person to know about it. What'smore, I'll phone you as soon as I get the result."

I wanted to tell Evans to fuck off but I was feeling too charitable to do so. At eight o'clock that morning, my phone rang again (I had forgotten to leave it off the hook). I heard Evans's voice:

"Charlie, old fellow, I've got fantastic news!"

"Oh?"

"I've spat into my handkerchief, and I've put the specimen under the microscope."

"Indeed?"

"It was N.M.C.S."

"What's that stand for?"

"No malignant cells seen!" shrieked Evans, "It means I haven't got carcinoma!"

"Great Scot!"

"Ah," the maniac went on, "don't think I'm going to be too trusting. I'm getting the tube to central London, and I'm going to make quite sure that the disease hasn't developed during my journey. I'll do another spit when I get to my office. There's a microscope there as well."

"Please don't phone me again unless it's positive," I said.

Evans said he'd try not to ring me again, but he did another of his spits and phoned me at nine o'clock on a Saturday morning when I was having a lie-in. I heard a hearty Welsh voice booming down the line.

"N.M.C.S!" Evans repeated over and over again, and even went so far as to sing these initials to the tune of Big Ben. I could sense that Evans was barking mad, so I changed my phone number, having suggested politely to him that he see a psychiatrist.

"After about eighteen months, I read in the *Daily Express* that someone known as Leslie Evans had just died. The article said that a man by that name, an eccentric dwarf, who once worked in the post-mortem room at Bede's Hospital in London, had had a pathological fear of dying, and more importantly, of becoming ill. Apparently, Evans had bought a series of medical books about different ways of dying, as well as books about fatal illnesses. He had put shelves up above his bed to support these books.

According to the article in the *Daily Express*, the shelves had given way under the weight of the books and had killed him.

Charlie told all his friends this story. Trout, Annabella and I laughed. Trout gave his characteristic laugh, sounding like an old-fashioned typewriter carriage return.

"I don't like that story, one bit" said the Professor. "I think it's damned sick. I can't abide black humour."

"Thanks a bloody heap!" said Esmerelda. Her drugs were beginning to wear off, and she was starting to feel the withdrawal symptoms. The Professor rang for Sister McNabe who sent for the orderlies, to hold Esmerelda down while she gave her her injection.

She later told the Professor a few more of Charlie's stories.

Stiffs Part Three

I was told to do a temporary booking in St Theresa's Hospital in Fulham. I was asked to work in the mortuary there, I was unnerved when I turned up because the woman in charge was very rude.

The mortuary was contained in a red-brick, dome-like building, not far from the hospital itself.

To enter my place of work, I had to bang repeatedly on an extremely thick door. I could hear an angry woman shouting on the other side of the door but she could not hear me knocking. She shouted:

"Are you doing anything on the evening of Monday, November 10th?" I made a mental note of the fact that it was then only early July. The woman had a thick Cockney accent.

"Are you doing anything on the evening of Tuesday, November 11th?"

"Oh," I heard the woman say gloomily. She still failed to hear me banging on the door.

"Are you doing anything on the evening of Wednesday, November 12th?"

I used this opportunity to kick the door hard. I was suddenly reminded of an incident during my school days, when I was thrown out of the Shakespeare Society: I was playing the part of the Porter in Macbeth. Among other things, I had to say, "Who's there in the name of Beelzebub. I started asking who was there, before the person who was supposed to be knocking, had turned up. I was seized by paroxysms of hysterical giggles, while the parents of the boys in the audience grumbled discontentedly, and the curtain had to be lowered.

While I was waiting for the woman to open the door leading to the mortuary, I was still in a very giggly state. Nerves. Nothing else. Just nerves.

"Let's get this straight," I heard the woman say to the henpecked person at the other end of the line. "Is it that you can't see me, or is it that you don't want to see me, if you can possibly avoid it?"

A pause was followed by an earth-shattering shout: "What the hell do you mean, the latter? You've been sleeping with me, dammit". The shouting went on, "Who's that knocking on the door? Well, I suppose I'll have to put the bloody phone down now. It'll be the fucking undertakers!"

Once again, I was reminded of the Porter incident, and the more nervous I got, the more I giggled. I wasn't looking forward to meeting this woman, because I feared that she would take her misfortunes out on me and send me home without my earnings.

"She opened the door by throwing her whole weight against it. I lowered my head and smiled at her.

"She looked like a tart. She had short, pitch black hair, cut in a fringe and was wearing a bright red mini dress. She looked about fifty years old.

"Who the hell are you?" she demanded.

"I'm Charles Yates. I'm from Manpower Services, and I understand you need a hand over here for the next month or so. Just tell me what to do and I will do it gladly. Isn't it lovely weather?"

The woman didn't look at me but at the floor. Then she looked out of the window at the sun in the azure blue sky.

"Your wish is my command," I said, with lamb-like meekness. "I understand that the Crighton who works for you normally, has gone to Lourdes in search of a cure for deep depression."

The woman showed no interest in what I had to say.

"Let the undertakers in and give them the key to the freezer!" she commanded peremptorily, without averting her gaze from the floor.

That was about all I could take. I was struck yet again by paroxysms of laughter, which I tried to disguise by coughing and making excuses about asthma.

The woman wasn't taken in by my excuses, however. "Don't just stand there sniggering, boy!" she shouted, "Let the buggers in!"

"I'm afraid there's no one out there," I said.

"Yes, there is, you blind fart! Let them in and give them the key to the bloody freezer."

"I've only just got here and I don't know where the key to the freezer is kept," I said.

"Only just got here, eh? Instructions were given last Friday for someone to be sent here at nine o'clock this morning and it's now nearly ten o'clock."

"I have been waiting outside, hatless, in the scorching sun since nine o'clock this morning. It wasn't my fault." I said.

"If you had been out there, why the hell didn't you knock on the door?" asked the woman.

"I knocked repeatedly but you didn't hear me. It would appear that you were on the phone."

She looked at me with slight embarrassment and produced from a box a bulky object which only Frankenstein would have used to let his creatures out of their cages with. She hurled the key in my direction, hitting me hard on the foot. I opened the door and saw two slovenly-looking men, wearing frayed jeans and tennis shoes but no undertakers. I was becoming very upset by this time.

I asked the two men whether they had seen any undertakers, expecting to find someone dressed in a pin-striped suit and a top hat. Surprisingly, one of the men said that they *were* undertakers. That didn't mean funeral directors but general odd job men who worked in undertakers' shops.

"The same spoke with a London accent. The other spoke with a north-country accent. The northerner did most of the talking.

"You bet yer fairce I'm a bloody oondertaiker!" he said and added that he and his mate had been waiting outside in the blinding heat for about half an hour.

I let the two scruffy-looking men into the mortuary. The northerner advanced towards the woman in charge and pinched her on the bottom. She did not seem to mind. The Londoner followed suit. Then the freezers were opened and their contents were exposed.

"Oh, *do* call me, 'Maggie', both of you," she said to the men, adding, "all my fellas call me that. You, too, can call me, 'Maggie'", she said to me, while the two ruffians were putting the bodies into coffins. She added, "You're so meek and gentle, and you didn't answer me back when I was offhand towards you."

"You seemed awfully stressed out," I said. "Is there a reason for this?"

"Of course there's a bloody reason for this," said Maggie. "One of my psychiatrists is in Los Angeles. The other's in Scotland. Incidentally, you *will* come back next week, won't you?"

"No, I won't. I'm not even staying for the day. You're too rude."

That's the last I ever saw of a mortuary. The work – sorry about the cliché, folks – is dead boring.

"I didn't like that story either, Esmerelda," said the Professor. He added disdainfully, "The *Macbeth* references were reasonably funny. I wish Charlie's stories were like that. I suppose the other stories you told me made me feel really sick."

"In that case, Professor, when I tell you Charlie's other stories, perhaps you should bring a sick-basin with you," said Esmerelda coldly. She had taken a violent dislike to the Professor.

Another of Charlie's Stories

How Mr and Mrs Pleasuredog Spent Christmas Eve

In the village where my mother lives, there's an old manor house. Its ownership and humorous anecdotes have been passed on through generations. The house is just outside Winslow in Buckinghamshire. The Lord and Lady of the Manor were titled. They were youngish to middle-aged, but my mother said you couldn't tell whether they were in their thirties or fifties. The Lord of the Manor was a kindly, good-humoured man. He was the Editor of the *Buckinghamshire Echo*. He and his wife were said to be cultured, to have travelled extensively, and to have had a continental look about them. They had two twin daughters, aged eight.

My mother heard the following story about two retainers in the village who had once worked for the Lord and Lady of the Manor. On their retirement, they lived in a cottage near the manor house. In his heyday, the man had been a gardener. His wife had been a cleaner and her name was Mrs Pleasuredog.

"That's a damned silly name!" interrupted the Professor.

"Every Christmas Day, the Lord and Lady of the Manor visited the cottages inhabited by their retainers and my mother says they were known to be very generous. They gave all their retainers Christmas presents. If it was a retainer with a child, they gave the child a bicycle, that sort of thing.

Apart from the other retainers, the Lord and Lady of the Manor got saddled with having to visit the eccentric Mrs Pleasuredog, who was in her eighties.

When they knocked at her door, Mrs Pleasuredog opened it, wearing her white hair in curlers, a dressing gown and carpet slippers on this occasion she was sobbing her guts out.

"And a *very* happy Christmas to you, Mrs Pleasuredog!" the Lord and Lady of the Manor said in unison, pretending they had not noticed that anything was amiss.

"Oh, your Lordship! Your Ladyship! I can't tell you how moved I am by your having called at my cottage. It means so very much to me, after what I had to go through last night. Oh, your Ladyship!…"

To the mortification of the Lord of the Manor, Mrs Pleasuredog knelt down at his feet, like a serf begging for bread in the Middle Ages.

"Please stand up, Mrs Pleasuredog," the Lord of the Manor said, "The surface of the ground is cold at this time of year." He helped Mrs Pleasuredog to her feet.

"Oh, your Lordship, if only you could have *seen* what happened last night."

"What happened last night, Mrs Pleasuredog?" the Lord of the Manor forced himself to ask, while the Lady of the Manor tried to encourage her with a radiant smile.

"It was my husband. The asylum said that he could come home for Christmas, and he's no better. He woke me up in the middle of the night, dragged me out of bed, and then he tied me up and did me in the garden shed!"

"That shed, the one over there?" asked the Lord of the Manor, not knowing what else to say in the circumstances.

"That shed!" sobbed Mrs Pleasuredog. The Lord of the Manor looked briefly at the shed and then at the Lady of the Manor who told her twin daughters to go off and play.

"It sounds as if you had a most harrowing and indeed

ghastly night," the Lord of the Manor forced himself to say. He wondered what he'd done in the last incarnation to get landed up in a situation like this. Quite apart from having to visit this nutty old cleaner, his spirits were that much lower than usual this year. This was due to a printers strike on the *Buckinghamshire Echo*, which had already lost over ten thousand copies. His attention swiftly returned to Mrs Pleasuredog.

"You see," she wept, "it's not the fact that he *did* me that I'm complaining about, or even that he wanted to do me at my age. It was the fact that he found it necessary to drag me out of bed and tie me up in a shed to do me. I mean, he was always so kind and considerate towards me when we was young. Even when we was courting, he didn't go beyond a kiss and a cuddle."

The Lord of the Manor blushed to the roots of his hair, and bent over to tie up his shoe laces which he had to untie, in order to tie up again. Then he began fiendishly to practice his golf swing, something which he always did when he was embarrassed.

"I do so hope the new year will prove to be a happier one than this one, Mrs Pleasuredog," said the Lady of the Manor, with her customary radiant smile. She tried as easily as she could, to back out of Mrs Pleasuredog's presence, before being interrupted.

"No one seems to realize that I am eighty-four years old," said Mrs Pleasuredog, "and I'm sure I look as if I was in my late nineties."

"I can assure you that you certainly don't look a day over sixty," the Lord of the Manor forced himself to remark, "and how old is Mr Pleasuredog?"

"Eighty-nine."

"Then, if you don't mind my saying so, he must be remarkably strong for an eighty-nine-year-old."

It was then possible to see a fleeting image of Mr Pleasuredog through the living-room window. He was wearing shabby, brown corduroy trousers, an equally shabby, beige duffle coat and a black woollen hat. He was putting something onto a Christmas tree. When he saw that he had visitors to his cottage, he waved, smiling imbecilically, and continued with what he was doing. He only had one tooth which had decayed.

The Lady of the Manor went into auto-pilot. "And a *very* happy Christmas and new year to you both," she said. She handed an envelope to Mrs Pleasuredog and backed out of her presence. The Lord of the Manor did the same thing.

Mrs Pleasuredog, who had just been given a fat cheque, closed the front door of her cottage and continued to sob, despite the money which she had received.

The Professor continued to type on his word processor.

"Charlie sure did know how to tell a sordid story when he wanted to," he, said, adding, "That story gave me the creeps. It shows that you have abysmal tastes and equally abysmal friends."

Esmerelda fixed the Professor with a vicious sneer and pulled her blankets up to her neck.

Another of Charlie's Stories

How Kevin Flanagan Disgraced Himself at the Manor House

The same witness told me another story about an incident in the lives of the Lord and Lady of the Manor.

Kevin Flanagan, a barrister, had been invited to dinner there. He's a manic depressive. When he's depressed, there's little of note to record about his behavior, but when he's manic, by God, he's manic! When he's on form, he can get his clients off, even if they've committed first degree murder, but if he's having one of his turns, his clients are only fortunate if they like the taste of porridge.

He took all his clothes off on a golf course once, because he thought that nakedness would improve his play. Then he banged on the front door of a clergyman's house and shouted, "Clothes! Clothes please! My need is greater than yours!" Another time when he was manic, he took all his clothes off in Westminster Abbey. When the police came to arrest him, he sang a ribald song to the tune of *The British Grenadiers:*

"Some talk of Alexander and some of Hercules,
Of Hector and Lysander and poofters such as these,
But of all the fucking pederasts, there's none that can compare,
With a bloody effeminate copper and a wanking raging queer."

When he went to dinner at the manor house, he was manic and also pretty inebriated. Although he was expected at eight o'clock, he arrived at eleven-thirty. The Lord and Lady of the Manor were waiting for him in the drawing room. The Lady of the Manor was lying on a maroon velvet sofa. Her dark hair, eyes and high cheek bones were accentuated by a flattering angle-poise lamp. She was angry and bored and was reading the *New Statesman*. "God, Hamlet was such a maddening young man!" she remarked, half to herself and half out loud.

Flanagan kicked open a door which banged against a table, knocking over a framed photograph of the Lady of the Manor's father, whom she had idolized. Flanagan ignored the Lady of the Manor and staggered drunkenly towards the Lord of the Manor and Editor of the *Buckinghamshire Echo*, who was sitting in an armchair in a corner of the room, his facial expression stern, his eyebrows raised and his eyes questioning.

"Not a bad rag, the *Echo*, what!" Flanagan boomed, slapping his thigh, "some of the sub-editors' wives are bloody good fucks!"

The Lord of the Manor, who was very easily shocked, even in the tamest of circumstances, was struck dumb, and looked as if he were about to faint. The Lady of the Manor, who was well-known for her ready wit, her sharp tongue and her quick temper, was also struck dumb.

She had been forewarned of Flanagan's recurrent mental illness, but she still took a little while to recover her senses.

"Why in the world are you so late?" she asked mildly.

"My car broke down, blast it!" said Flanagan, pouring himself a drink, "I was going to get the bastard fixed but the mechanic who said he'd do it, got carted off to hospital with V.D. " Flanagan drained his glass, poured himself another and repeated the procedure.

Strangely, the Lady of the Manor decided to let this ride,

and an uncomfortable silence ensued, which was broken by the entry of Jones, the butler, who came in to refill Flanagan's glass.

"Oh, don't go filling his glass up, Jones, for mercy's sake!" the Lady of the Manor pleaded frantically, a strong note of hysteria in her voice. "He's already worked his way through three great big brimming beakers of Bacardi." Jones shuffled awkwardly out of the room, looking anxiously from left to right, as if he were crossing a busy road, and quietly closed the door behind him. Jones, too, had had a few too many.

"What is the matter with your car?" the Lady of the Manor asked Flanagan.

"It's the points. They need greasing."

"In that case, you should grease your points regularly, shouldn't you, Mr Flanagan?"

Another surge of mania swept through Flanagan.

"I'll grease my points! I'll grease 'em all right!" he shouted, pacing up and down the room, like an expectant father, "and if you're a good girl, I'll take you upstairs to your bedroom and I'll give your points a good old greasing!"

The Lady of the Manor's fiercely quick tongue was anaesthetized yet again, and another silence ensued before she spoke.

"I don't think this is the sort of conversation that one expects to have in a *William Kent* drawing room," she said, while the Lord of the Manor stared, transfixed, as if he had seen a vision.

"*William Kent*! *William* bloody *Kent*! Never 'eard of the wet fucker!" shrieked Flanagan. The Lord of the Manor suddenly came to his senses.

"Will you kindly leave my house this instant!" he shouted, while the Lady of the Manor, who was actually more frightening than her husband, sprang to her feet and chased Flanagan into the hall.

"Go back to the bog and take your filthy manners with

you!" she yelled, and accompanied her outburst by a stream of furious abuse which was, interestingly, devoid of swear words, which anyone in a similar situation would have been tempted to use.

Flanagan grabbed hold of a bright red overcoat, which had been left on a chair in the hall. Quite undaunted by the fury of the Lady of the Manor, he picked it up and chased her round the hall table, singing at the top of his voice.

"Toreador en garde. Toreador, toreador."

He waved the coat in front of the Lady of the Manor, skipping from one foot to the other with the agility of a matador.

The Lady of the Manor realized that their roles had been alarmingly reversed. She was no longer chasing Flanagan. Flanagan was chasing her. He continued to chase her round in circles for about five minutes. Although the Lady of the Manor had always been an active athlete, Flanagan was moving too fast for her. His mad, staring eyes were scaring her out of her wits. Somehow, she managed to escape through the nearest door, and turned the key behind her.

"I was told that this was the only time in her life that she had actually feared for her safety.

The Professor dusted his computer screen.

"I suppose that's a fractionally amusing story, Esmerelda" he said, in a cutting tone of voice. Adding, "but I bet it's not true."

"It bloody well *is* true," said Esmerelda defensively. "You really are an obnoxious man!"

Another of Charlie's Stories

The Strange Solicitors

During my holidays, I worked as a solicitor's clerk in indescribably filthy rooms in Camberwell, London, S.E.5.. The solicitors practised under the name of H.E.L.H. Hurecholedo and Partner. The firm consisted of a middle-aged man called Henry Edward Laurence Huan Hurecholedo, an extraordinary mixture of Spanish and English names, and a woman in her fifties called Mildred Jenkins. They were forever shouting and screaming at each other. They permanently claimed professional one-upmanship over the other. They constantly blamed each other for the proverbial seediness to which their practice had sunk.

Mildred was fat, badly dressed and had frizzy, unmanageable grey hair, which grew to her shoulders and which was never washed. Hurecholedo was almost as fat as Mildred. He rarely washed his clothes. You did not need scrambled eggs for breakfast. All you needed to do was to suck his waistcoat.

They often threw things at each other on the stairs, even if a client happened to be staggering upstairs, clinging to the banisters which came away in his hands. The luckless client's attention was sometimes distracted by an ashtray overflowing with three weeks' worth of cigarette ends. This flew past his head and sometimes hit it.

"Oh, rubbish!" muttered the Professor.

Esmerelda ignored him and continued to tell Charlie's story.

I used to put Valium into the solicitors' tea. When they got used to the five milligram dose, I raised it to ten milligrams, and from ten milligrams to thirty milligrams, etc. I was putting at least sixty milligrams into their tea by the time I left them. You may call my conduct unethical. I would like to see you trying to work in an office for three or four hours at a time, with two maniacs screaming at the tops of their voices just outside it.

When I wasn't in my office or in the magistrates' court, my job was to accompany the Bailiff on his rounds, while he served writs on mad or violent husbands. Sometimes, the husbands were forbidden to walk within two hundred yards of their terrified, cowering wives. My function at the Bailiff's side was that of a witness, in case the person on whom the writ was being served, became violent. This happened quite often.

The Bailiff's name was Terry Brown. He was supposed to serve a writ on a particularly violent defendant called John Walker. Walker had forced his wife to have unnatural sex with him, because she had refused him ordinary sex. When she showed her disgust by becoming hysterical, he pushed a broom handle into her body, so she went to stay with her sister.

"The Bailiff had some trouble finding the right doorbell, as the names on all the bells had been scratched away by vandals. He rang the bell which he thought was John Walker's bell and we were both surprised to see an eccentric old lady, opening the door.

She had on a black shimmering evening gown and dainty shoes, as if she were going to a ball. When she let us into her flat, she showed neither self- consciousness about her appearance, nor even the slightest interest in John Walker. She ignored us both, and continued her act of putting a golf ball into a rubber boot turned on its side.

A man suddenly emerged from behind a screen. He was about fifteen years younger than the old lady, and was dressed as if he were about to embark on a stormy trek across the Yorkshire moors.

"This is Jeff," the old lady said in a loud, hoarse tone of voice. She had a powerful, upper class accent. She added, "He's the man who holds my head while I'm being sick, which happens at least three times a day, what with my dreadful old spleen." At this point, her heavy upper class accent became even stronger.

"Does he need to wear fisherman's waders, an oilskin and a sou'wester for this purpose?" the Bailiff asked rudely. He then asked the old lady if she knew where John Walker lived.

"Oh, that ghastly oik!" the old lady replied, "He lives in the flat just above mine and shoves things into his wife, the damned kinky bugger! I haven't got the time of day for any of that damned bloody rubbish! I'm a colonial, though you wouldn't know it. Brought up in Honkers, I was. I had servants who brought me tea and gin and tonic by the swimming pool. I haven't got time to discuss the damned rubbish that's always going on upstairs."

"May I take your name, please?" said Brown.

"Lady Dorothea de Florence."

He thanked her and went upstairs. There was an overpowering smell of stale urine on the frayed threadbare carpet. A lavatory in a filthy condition was broken and the lock on the door had been smashed. When Brown rang Walker's bell, Walker came to the door with half a bottle of whisky in his hand and tried to smash it over his head, but Brown leapt out of the way.

"It's a shame to waste good whisky," I ventured. Walker then threw the bottle in my direction but missed and fell over. While Walker was recuperating after his momentary loss of balance, Brown pressed the writ into his hand.

When I got back to the offices, I found the Walker versus Walker file and was amused by the use of understatements in the Petitioner's Particulars of Claim. Until then, I had been ignorant about legal matters and the use of legal jargon. One paragraph in the Walker versus Walker file read as follows:

'On 6th May, 1980, the Respondent, in another hysterical rage, banged his fists on the kitchen table in the matrimonial home, and smashed a bottle of rum, putting the Petitioner in fear of a violent fate upon her. The Respondent told her that if she did not submit to each of his requests, of a violent and sexually perverse nature, he would kill her, whereby the Petitioner suffered humiliation and distress…'

Each clause of the Petitioner's Particulas of claim ended with these words.

One morning, I went into Mildred Jenkins's office, and told her that I had to go to the magistrates' court with Mr Hurecholedo that afternoon.

"Bad luck," she said, "you've my full sympathy."

"But I *like* going to the magistrates' court with Mr Hurecholedo."

"I see," Mildred replied acidly, "I suppose you like watching all his clients go down with six months!"

"I wasn't thinking about it from that point of view," I said, "Mr Hurecholedo reminds me of Rumpole of the Bailey, once he gets going in court."

"At least, Rumpole won a case, once in a while," shouted Mildred and walked out of her office, slamming the door behind her.

* * *

Another of my jobs when working for the solicitors, was to man the phones and if necessary, let clients in, while the solicitors were at court.

I opened the door to a woman who would have made an elephant look like a midget. She looked about forty years old. She was unwashed and had not changed her clothes for about a month. Her foul odour blended unpleasantly with the lingering smell of body odour and generalized rot in Mr Hurecholedo's office. The fat, dirty client took a seat in what in better days had been a waiting-room. Most of the upholstery of the chairs had been hacked out by clients' knives and there were no taps in the sink, where a pile of washing-up had accumulated. The sink had been wrenched away from the wall by some of Mr Hurecholedo's more violent clients.

"Everybody's out," I said to the verminous creature sitting in the waiting room. "However, I'll take all your details. Stand over there by the window and open it, will you. I suffer from asthma," I lied.

The woman opened the window and I noticed a slight improvement in the smell. I also noticed, from the overhead light which shone onto her face, that she had a repellent skin disorder, so I made up my mind not to look at her but beyond her.

"I've been living with a madman for two years," she began. (He'd have had to be off his rocker to want to live with her for two minutes, thought I, but I let her continue) "He's so violent. He comes home drunk and beats me with a hose pipe. The flat is rented by us jointly, but I've got nowhere to stay. Every time I go near him, he says he's going to kill me!"

"I've got something else I ought to show you," she said ominously. "Is there a table without anything on it, that I can strip and spread myself out on?"

"I began to tidy the desk in Mr Hurecholedo's office, and cleared away the ashtrays and the mountain of files from which Affidavits, Briefs to Counsel, Conveyances, Last Wills and Testaments etc. had accumulated into mountainous heaps of disorder.

"We'll need something to spread over the desk, first," the woman said mildly. I found Mr Hurecholedo's copy of *The Guardian* on the floor, opened it and laid it over the desk with its front page facing upwards. I noticed in passing that although we were then in the middle of a General Election campaign, there was an interminable story about the R.S.P.C.A. on the front page, and very little about the Election itself. Typical of *The Guardian*, thought I.

The woman lay down and pulled up her dress.

"What is your name?" I asked, covering my mouth with my hand.

"Margaret Scott."

"And your date of birth?"

"The first of October, 1952.

"What's your address?"

"The basement flat, 346 Albany Road, London, S.E.5.."

"I looked at Marigold's hideous naked body, but was too nauseated to do so for long.

"Your injuries are such that you need a gynaecologist, not a layman like me. I'm sorry, Mrs Scott but there is really nothing I can do to help you," I said. "I'll pass your details to Mr Hurecholedo." I went downstairs and opened the front door for her. I held the door open with one hand and covered my mouth, to hold back the bile, with the other.

* * *

I did not last in the solicitors' office for long. After being there for a month, the overpowering filth in the place became so unbearable that I decided to clean everything little by little one afternoon, when the solicitors were at court. I started on Mr Hurecholedo's room, and after throwing away the rotten food, used tins, bread crusts, cigarette stubs, etc. that had accumulated over about six months, I began to clear out the drawers. The first thing I saw was a long bloodstained knife with a jagged blade, on which dried blood had accumulated. By the knife, lay a coil of rope which was also covered with blood.

It seemed to me that both the rope and the knife had been left there for so long that neither could, in my opinion, have served any useful purpose. I bought a scrubbing brush, some disinfectant, some bleach and a plastic bucket from a local chemist. I soaked the offending articles in the plastic bucket and scrubbed them until the blood had disappeared without trace.

Two days later, the office was in an uproar. Mr Hurecholedo was walking up and down the dilapidated staircase, beating his brow and shouting,

"What the hell's happened to Exhibits T.B.1 and T.B.2 in the Proverbs versus Patterson case?" he screamed like one demented, adding "I'm meant to be representing Mr Proverbs, who was given up for dead, after being attacked by Patterson with the knife and rope. It's about the only case I'll ever make anything out of in my life, and some fucker's been in my office and washed the blood off the exhibits!"

I learnt through reading the file on the Proverbs versus Patterson case, that Gaslighter Tincan Proverbs was the man prosecuting he was black. He had settled in London. His first name was taken from a shop next door to his parents' apartment in Harlem, in which he was born. His middle name had some connection with the film, *The Wizard of Oz.*

His opponent, Clive Patterson, was a vicious, supporter of the National Front. He and Proverbs lived in adjacent flats in south London.

"The fight between the two men was triggered off by a disagreement about the ownership of a television set. It belonged to Proverbs, but Patterson claimed that it was his. Patterson picked up a long knife with a jagged blade and slashed Proverbs deeply on the back of the head with it. He had meant to slit his adversary's throat, but he got into a frenzy and lost his head.

On the knife, was a marked dent, showing where it had collided with the black man's skull. Patterson finally tried to strangle Proverbs with the rope and, left hideous welts round his neck, having broken his skin. Hence, both the rope and the blade of the knife had been covered with blood.

"This really is the end! It's just not fair!" Hurecholedo wailed wretchedly, "I was so certain I would win this case that I promised my wife I would take her to the south of France, where she's never been in her life. I was going to take her to Cannes, to Nice, to St Tropez..." His shouting voice turned into a sob.

Eventually, I confessed my deed to Mr Hurecholedo. I resigned before he had an opportunity to sack me. I felt guilty beyond belief.

The Professor furiously slapped his laptop shut. He was silent for a while. Eventually, he said, "This story of is absolutely nauseating. The more you tell me, Esmerelda, the less I like Charlie. He seems to have thrived on the suffering of others."

"You're quite wrong about Charlie," said Esmerelda angrily. "He only laughed because he saw that there was a funny side to all things grave."

"So you call filth all over someone's offices funny, do you? Also, Charlie appeared to be amused by the fact that a solicitor was being denied the holiday of a life time. You, too, seem to find it funny."

"Yes, I bloody well do find it funny, well, most of it anyway," said Esmerelda, her voice raised. Of course, there has to be a funny side to all things grave, as I said earlier. Charlie indulged in black humour; he was just trying to prove his theory."

"I can't abide black humour, as I said before and I can't tolerate people wasting my time," said the Professor disagreeably.

"Tell me your next Charlie story if you must, Esmerelda. Kindly make sure it's going to be a lot more wholesome than the ones you've told me recently. The Charlie stories you've told me so far are plain sick, particularly the one about the solicitors."

"OK, Prof, the next story's wholesome, scouts honour," said Esmerelda cheekily.

Another of Charlie's Stories

The Indiscretions of the Reverend Boyne, —
Incorporating the Burial of Sir Edmund Card

I've got an old friend who lives in Cornwall and who is Cornish. His name is Barrus Elliott. He has always regarded himself as being a man of the sea. His greatest happiness is found at the helms of sailing boats, raging through violent waters. However, at the time of this story, he had personal troubles and his circumstances had forced him to stay on shore. He is physically very strong and he became a grave-digger. Barrus had a brother called Bert. Bert's best friend was called Nat Jago.

Everyone hated Nat Jago, including Barrus. His brother, Bert, who was very frail, having been invalided out of the Merchant Navy was suffering from pneumonia. Nat went to his house while he was infectious with a heavy cold. He gave his germs to Bert and caused his death. Even Barrus, who was so good-natured, hated Nat's guts.

It's very easy to get on well with Barrus. His principal axiom is, "Never make an enemy if you can possibly make a friend." Whatever job he does, however menial it may be, he does it conscientiously, unless someone is abusive towards him.

Even the Reverend Boyne, who had long ago lost the respect of his parishioners, due to the disgusting language he used during moments of frustration, took a liking to Barrus, and always offered him a swig of whisky from his hip flask, while the two men were waiting for undertakers to turn up.

"This fucking bloody mob never get their fat asses here on time!" the Reverend Boyne shouted one day to Barrus, who was leaning patiently on his spade. " 'Ere, get some of this shit down your skull!"

Barrus observed that funeral directors seldom accompanied their staff to the cemetery except in unusual circumstances. The only firm personally represented by its director, was Trevor Pengelly and Sons, which was run by a universally disliked man called Trevor Pengelly. Even Barrus, who gets on with almost everybody, had a particular dislike for Pengelly, who patronized him and addressed him as "boy", and in some cases even, as "lackey", within the hearing of others.

Barrus found a way of causing grief and embarrassment to Pengelly. Hence, Pengelly never came back to the same cemetery ever again.

The funeral was that of a Lord Mayor. His name was Sir Edmund Card and he was highly respected within the community .

All his relatives were present, namely his wife, his ex-wife, his children by both his marriages, his cousins and his grandchildren. The church was completely full. Some mourners had to stand outside the church.

"Make sure you get this one right, lackey," Pengelly shouted to Barrus, just before Sir Edmund's burial.

"With pleasure, I'll get it right for you, Squire, and I'll put a move on you, first."

Barrus took Pengelly under the arm in a complex wrestling move, known only to Cornishmen. Pengelly who came from the border of Devon and Cornwall, had no charity towards the underdog. Fell to his knees and groaned with pain.

"There's worse I'll do to you, yet, Squire," said Barrus, "because you called me 'lackey', a few too many times."

A heavy thunderstorm came on, but Barrus got on with his job, which was to dig Sir Edmund's grave. He only allowed for five feet seven and a half inches, instead of the five feet eleven inches which the luckless Sir Edmund Card required. Barrus rested on his spade and waited. Pengelly knew nothing of Barrus's revenge. His team put the webbing under Sir Edmund's coffin but they were unable to lower it into the grave. Pengelly barked orders at Elliott.

"Rectify the situation, Lackey!" he shouted.

Barrus obeyed the order and rectified himself in the clumsiest and most irreverent manner imaginable. He introduced a lot of play acting into his performance. He told the pall bearers to drag the webbing upwards, and the coffin, containing Sir Edmund Cards body to be laid down on the earth just outside the grave.

Barrus got into the grave once more, and violently dug out more earth. He dug, and dug and dug. A lot of the time he inadvertently threw spadesful of earth into the faces of Sir Edmund Card's loved ones.

* * *

However, Barrus wasn't the only person to disgrace himself at Pengelly's funerals.

Pengelly's firm was replaced by a firm called Crumblebottom and Bongwit.

Suddenly, the Reverend Bernard Boyne rolled up his sleeve and gave himself a heroin injection, while he was reciting prayers by the grave of the person who had just been buried.

As he was leaving the cemetery, chuckling and muttering to himself out loud, the hearse pulled up alongside him. Crumblebottom, the new funeral director, wound down his window and leant out.

"Couldn't you have had your injection at some other time?" he asked mildly.

"No," replied the Reverend Boyne assertively.

"There is blood on your garments. How did it get there? I demand to be told," said Crumblebottom.

"The spike screwed up on me. When I shoot up, I usually do a clean job."

"What the blazes do you mean, when you shoot up?" rasped Crumblebottom.

"I'm on heroin and it's suckers like me, who keep fuckers like you in business."

"You're a sheer, utter disgrace to your cloth."

"What the fucking hell do you think it's for?" shouted the Reverend Boyne.

"You told me that your next story wouldn't be unwholesome, Esmerelda," barked the Professor. "You lied to me, didn't you?"

"I sure did, Professor," said Esmerelda, smiling. She added, "Not only that most of the story's *not* unwholesome. You're just a reactionary with no sense of humour. Why don't you become a monk?"

The Strange Ways of the French (in the Eyes of the English)

When I was living in Paris, I took pleasure in attending the *Palais de Justice*. I was sitting in the crowded public gallery, and was amused by the exchanges between the presiding magistrate and the occupants of the dock.

The presiding magistrate's name was Jean-Cédric Gautier. (That was not his real name.) He was drunk but dapper, with neatly-cut, dark hair, parted at the side. The cases he was in charge of took place after he had had what must have been a pretty liquid lunch. He stumbled as he entered the courtroom and staggered into his chair, singing under his breath:

""Au clair de la lune – e

Je pétais dans l'eau.

Ça faisait des boules – e.

C'etait rigolo."[3*]

He fidgetted while in his chair, and rubbed his hands with glee as he surveyed the defendants sitting in front of him.

"Delighted to see you, my children," he remarked (in French). His accent was obscenely Parisian. A Parisian accent sounds like a filthy old Arab, cleaning his teeth with a lavatory brush.

3 [*]*"In the light of the moon,*
*I f***** in the water.*
It made bubbles.
It was hilarious."

He continued, "It is your crimes that give me the right to work."

The two defendants were a married couple in their early sixties, from the "sixteenth" district of Paris (le *seizième arrondissement*). The man was dressed like a suburban bank manager, and his wife was wearing an imitation fur coat and a matching fur hat. They were accused of leaving a restaurant without paying the bill (which incidentally was very modest). The paucity of the sum irritated Gautier. He had no patience for the owner of the restaurant, who was the first to give evidence.

The restaurant owner made an elaborate speech about how he had chased the couple out of the restaurant, and how he had eventually made a citizen's arrest in the street. Gautier struggled to stay awake which wasn't easy after his heavy alcohol consumption.

"I'm listening, monsieur, I'm listening," he said, "with my head resting on the back of my chair and my eyes tightly closed, but I'm listening all the same."

The restaurant owner was irritated by Gautier's indifference and shouted his head off. Gautier, lost his temper.

"Do you mean you are wasting my time over such a modest sum?" he bellowed.

The couple's defence counsel intervened, shouting at the top of his voice and waving his arms in the air, like a swimmer calling for help. Gautier was the next one to shout.

"Monsieur thought that Madame had paid! Madame thought that Monsieur had paid! It was not a crime that they committed! It was no more than a mere misunderstanding, so shut up, the pair of you! By now, Gautier was so drunk that he seemed oblivious of his surroundings.

"He was fractionally more tolerant when he addressed the female defendant, who was very tearful and who stated that the incident was accidental. Gautier rubbed his hands together and shrugged his shoulders in a bemused Gallic gesture:

"Et c'est pour ça que nous nous rencontrons dans cette sale."[4*] It was clear that the alcohol was wearing off by this time.

"What struck me during my attendance at the *Palais de Justice* was the lack of bureaucracy and pomposity that make British courtroom scenes seem so pathetic. It's hard to imagine an English magistrate drunkenly losing his temper, with a witness who had been robbed of a ludicrously small sum of money.

"Last, but not least of the extraordinary eccentricity of the French, is how could anyone vote for a man like Le Pen? He can't even sing the *Marseillaise* in tune. How could anyone vote for his supporters, even?"

"That's a fractionally more amusing story, Esmerelda," muttered the Professor. He added, "It's devoid of the usual filth and smut that your sordid friend, Charlie, likes to put into his stories, solely in order to impress people."

Esmerelda didn't reply. She just gave the Professor a V sign.

4 [*] *And that is why we are meeting each other in this room.*

I Don't Want That Brat On My Boat, Ever Again

Here's another story about the eccentricity of the French. I was twelve years old. Albert, my brother, was older. We were staying in a villa in Cap d'Antibes with our father, a widower. Albert and I joined other visitors on a boat on which aqualung diving was taught. The captain of the boat was an over-excitable, hot-tempered Frenchman called Christian Malinet.

Relations between Malinet and myself were poor, even from the start. I was good at aqualung diving, and Malinet suggested to Albert and me that we dive about a hundred feet below water level to look at a wreck. He told us not to go into the wreck, in case our mouth pieces became punctuated by brushing against jagged edges.

I decided to deliberately disobey Malinet, not through malice, but for a purely perverse reason. I had noticed that whenever he swore, he shouted at the top of his voice and used an expression which was pure nectar to my ears and more wonderful than the rarest music ever composed. When Malinet was in a bait he didn't simply shout "*Merde!*" It had to be, "*Et puis, merde – e!*"[5*] Had he just said, '*Merde,*' I would not have insisted on provoking him.

Malinet was livid when he saw that I had swum into the

5 * *And then shi-it!*

wreck. He swam into the wreck, after me, and grabbed me by my arms and legs, took me to the "bends" barrier, about five feet below the surface of the water, and held me to the anchor chain. He waited for the different water pressures to settle, to prevent me from getting the "bends."

It is said that the bends can be fatal. It means the accumulation of nitrogen bubbles in the blood. It is said to be caused if a diver comes to the surface of the water too quickly.

I personally think that the "bends" is an old wives' tale. There have been frequent occasions when I have come to the surface of the water too quickly, and I've never caught the "bends".

On one occasion, I was drunk and my head hit the bottom of the boat during a mistral after. I had reached a hundred and twenty feet below the surface of the water and I felt sick. I needed to get to the surface of the water fast.

When I went down with Malinet this time, I wanted to hear an *et puis, merde – e* more than anything else in the world. The excitable Frenchman gesticulated with his arms to make me to get out of the water. I responded by waving my arms: No, I won't.

Malinet took me near the surface of the water and used ferocious sign language. He ordered me to get out. I indicated that I would not get out. Malinet was livid and turned my oxygen supply off. Thus, I was faced with two choices, either to come to the surface of the water immediately, or to take Malinet's mouthpiece out of his mouth and put it into my own.

I needed to breathe.

I chose the latter.

Malinet was probably homicidal. He pulled and pulled and pulled on his mouthpiece to get it out of my mouth, but my teeth were strong, and he couldn't do anything about it. While I was breathing happily and Malinet was fuming with rage, I made a circle with my thumb and index finger, which is the standard underwater signal for the words, "Are you all right?"

Once Malinet and I had scrambled onto the deck of the diving boat, I accidentally dropped my four-kilo weight belt onto his toe.

I was then able to rejoice in his glorious words, which were like pure honey being poured into my ears.

"*Et puis, merde – e!*" His voice was like a herd of stampeding elephants.

Albert came up the ladder a few minutes later. He had gone down with another instructor! Malinet stormed up to him, screaming in barrack room Marseillaise French. "I don't want that brat on my boat ever again!" he bellowed.

"Oh, why's that? Has he been naughty again?"

"Malinet swung his straightened arms round his head in deliciously comic fury, lashing the air like a windmill in a force ten gale. *"Et puis, merde – e!"* repeated the enchanting entertainer.

"Charlie was very naughty as a child," conceded the Professor. "He was hardly a paragon of virtue when he grew up, if he ever did grow up, which I very much doubt."

Another of Charlie's Stories

Picnic in the Rain

Here's a story about the eccentricity of the English, in the eyes of the French.

It is about two friends of my brother's, a man and his wife, who were both titled. They were called Lord and Lady Pendary. Lord Pendary had been given a life peerage sometime during Harold Wilson's government. He was a newspaper proprietor. His newspaper was, strictly speaking, a family paper.

On this occasion, Lord Pendary and his wife, Lady Pendary, were in a hotel in the south of France. They were staying in Cap d'Antibes and were expecting good weather, although weather conditions were poor.

"However, Lady Pendary had a bizarre *penchant* for having picnics in the rain. Lord Pendary disliked this but because his newspaper was selling well, he was good-natured and complied with his wife's wishes. Lady Pendary laughed at her husband's bizarre apparel. He had taken no chances. He was wearing a full-length black, plastic mackintosh and a matching sou'wester. He had also brought a bottle of whisky in the pocket of his mackintosh.

He allowed Lady Pendary to choose the venue. She chose the courtyard of a derelict villa to have lunch in. The Pendarys carried a hamper with two folded-up plastic chairs, and took the hamper and chairs into a red-tiled area, supported by grey stone pillars.

Lady Pendary opened the hamper and began to eat liver pâté, prawns, cold chicken and *brie*.

"This place is inhabited," said Lord Pendary suddenly. There's a man looking at us out of a window."

Lady Pendary went over to the man and spoke to him in French. "We won't be long. We'll be finished soon. We were told that this villa was unoccupied."

The man was too shy to answer and vaguely nodded his head. Lord and Lady Pendary lost interest in him and continued to eat.

Lady Pendary was unaware of the fact that the man had considered her and her husband to be completely mad and had called the *gendarmerie.*

"Lady Pendary had just finished her second glass of *rosé,* and was spreading butter and *brie* onto half a *baguette*. When she looked up, she saw three *gendarmes*, the heavy rain dripping from their caps, onto their faces. They were knocked sidewise by the sight of a couple having lunch in such dastardly weather conditions, and assumed automatically that they were English.

"What are you doing here?" asked one of the dumbfounded *gendarmes* mildly. (He did all the talking.) Lady Pendary replied in French. She had a blistering Churchillian accent which was more potent than a tropical midday sun.

"*Un gentil jean homme*[6*] said that it was quite all right for us to stay here, until we've finished our lunch."

"What young man? What did he look like?"

"How can I say? I only saw his head. Leave us in peace. *Il faut respectez l'heure de dèjeuner*[7+]."

"Best to leave them alone. They're completely round the bend," said the *gendarme* who did all the talking.

6 [*]A pleasant young man

7 [+]You should respect lunch-time

"It was at this point that Lord Pendary bent over and poured a generous amount of whisky into a plastic cup.

"Lady Pendary had become quite inebriated by this time. She threw herself into theatrical humour.

"*Mon mari est un Milord anglais très eccentrique,*"[8**] she boomed at the *gendarmes*, her Churchillian brogue more pronounced even than it had been earlier.

"The *gendarmes* decided not to prosecute. One of them was heard remarking, "*Ils sont typiquement anglais. Seulement les anglais mangent leur déjeuner dehors en plein orage!*""[9*]

"I always judge someone by the company they keep, even if it is their brother's company. This story is wholesome enough, but it's as boring as hell," criticized the Professor.

8 **My husband is a very eccentric English Lord."

9 *They're typically English. Only the English would eat their lunch outside in a raging storm!"

Another of Charlie's Stories

The boat which crashed into a restaurant

Here's yet another of Charlie's stories. Like the last one, it is about the eccentricity of the English (in the eyes of the French).

"My father, my brother, Albert and I were on a rather small sailing boat, which was known as the HMS *Hysteria*. Albert was the skipper. We were in the south of France. Albert was fifteen years old and I was ten years old.

On this occasion, we were on the HMS *Hysteria*, accompanied by a frisky Alsatian dog called Vichy. Vichy had a *penchant* for gin and tonic, and liked to run round the lunch table barking his head off.

A *mistral* was starting. Albert turned the boat round in a circle. Another gust of wind pushed it violently up the beach, crashing it into a restaurant full of diners.

While all this was going on, my father, who was wearing a long white bath towel dressing gown, was sitting on the side of the boat, reading. He was making notes in the margins of what he was reading, paying no attention to what was going on around him.

Albert shouted at the top of his voice, while a cynical French crowd giggled and made jokes about the peculiarity of the English.

"As you can see, we are in a crisis, so I'm going to appoint you all as officers." He pointed towards me. "You are officer in charge of the front, right hand rope."

"It's actually called the "starboard jib sheet," said my father peremptorily.

Albert pointed to me again, "You are officer in charge of that big piece of wood, swinging backwards and forwards and hitting everyone on the bloody head."

"He turned to my father: "Hey, you there, 'crew member'."

"I will *not* be addressed as 'crew member'!" shouted my father.

Albert ignored my father and continued to rant. "You are officer in charge of the tiller and see that it's to leeward."

My father lost his temper, which was rare for him as he was a mild-mannered man.

"I do wish you'd stop talking all this rubbish about officers, and concentrate instead on what's going on in the water, or on the beach, call it what you will."

Vichy, in the meantime, was licking two naked lesbians' bottoms.

What made the situation worse, was the fact that Albert and I were laughing hysterically.

"*Ils sont complétement foux, les anglais*,"[10*] said one of the occupants of the restaurant, into which the HMS *Hysteria* had crashed.

"That story, unlike most of Charlie's other stories, is quite funny in places," said the Professor. "It's a shame not all of his stories are like that," he added reluctantly.

10 *They're raving mad, the English.

Another of Charlie's Stories

At Least I Didn't Get Flu

Battle against O.C.D. (obsessive compulsive disorder)

I went to a prep school and shared a dormitory with about six other boys. There was a lot of flu about. The boy in the bed next door to mine had been stricken and was sick on the floor. When the matron stormed into the dormitory, I was gaping at the mess in mesmerized horror.

"Oh, my Gawd, did you make that mess, Yates, you barmy idiot?"

"No, matron."

"Get your face out of it, then, you morbid blighter!"

"Yes, matron."

The matron was in a fantastic bait. She said, "I suppose I'll have to go all the way downstairs and get the bumper." As she left the dormitory, she shouted obscurely, "If Jesus Christ had woken up in the middle of the night feeling sick, he would have taken the trouble to get up and go to the lavatory!"

"I don't think there *were* any lavatories in the days of Jesus Christ," I ventured.

"One more word out of you, Yates, all right!" shouted the matron.

So terrified was I of catching the boy's germs, that I bundled up all my bedclothes and climbed onto the roof, using the fire escape. It was early February, and the outside temperature was almost zero. Some people might have considered my behaviour to be a bit 'oirish', but I've never cared what other people have thought about me.

I lay on the roof, rolled up in my bedclothes, staring happily at the stars, and I rejoiced in the fact that the February wind was devoid of germs.

The next morning, I was admitted to hospital, having been seen on the roof by a passing gardener. I had been unconscious for a while, and had contracted pneumonia in both lungs.

I awoke with a euphoric smile.

"I can't tell you how pleased I am that I didn't catch that boy's flu!" I said happily.

The Professor smiled rather unpleasantly. "Charlie obviously had no common sense," he muttered. "I don't find stories like that at all funny. In fact, I don't find any of Charlie's stories funny."

Another of Charlie's Stories

Charlie's Twelve Oranges
Author's Further Battle Against O.C.D. continued

After I got ill, I was sent home for a month. When it was time for me to go back to school, my nanny gave me a crate of oranges. There were twelve oranges in all.

Some of my schoolfellows resented the fact that I had an entire crate of oranges to myself. I began to get very possessive about my oranges, and counted them every night before bedtime.

On the fourth night, I found that three oranges were missing.

I was mortified by a burning sense of injustice. One night, I sat in the larder, waiting to be visited by the boy who had dared to steal my oranges.

At half past ten, someone did come into the larder and because it was so dark, he couldn't see me. I waited for him to put his hand into the crate.

I turned on the light, and realized that my oranges were being stolen by a shithead called Jack Ellison.

"Oh, no, you don't, you little bastard! You came in here last night, as well, and you stole three of my oranges then, didn't you?" I said.

"I swear it wasn't me," he replied.

"Jack Ellison, You lie! You lie! You lie! You lie! You were seen coming into the larder last night. Also, I caught you in here just now, with your hand in the crate."

"It wasn't me. It was Power. I saw him with an orange in his dressing gown pocket last night," said Ellison.

"Do you know something?" I asked.

"What?"

"You'll go to prison one day. I know it in my bones."

I was sick with rage and injustice. All those oranges were meant to help me to overcome my pneumonia. I reported Jack Ellison to the housemaster the next day but he didn't take any notice of my complaint. Perhaps, he resented the fact that I had a crate of oranges to myself.

I was mortified by feelings of persecution.

My security doubled. I spent each night in the larder, counting my oranges. I sat there every night until the end of term.

"I spent so much time counting my oranges, that I never got round to eating any of them.

"This man, Charlie, was raving mad!" commented the Professor unsympathetically, adding, "It's obvious that he didn't spend any time on his studies. He must have been very poorly educated when he grew up, if he *did* ever grow up, as I said once before."

Another of Charlie's Stories

Author's battle against O.C.D.: continued
My brother is always right.
How I Saved London

When I was six years old, I believed everything I was told by my elder brother, Albert, who was eleven years old. We were sitting in the garden at our Berkshire house. It was some months after the Cuban crisis.

We had houses in London and Berkshire. Every Friday, my father drove us to Berkshire. We spent the weekends in the country. My father was a journalist. My mother was dead. She had died in a plane crash. I was only two years old when she died.

My father inherited a certain amount from his father who was also a journalist. He, too, inherited a lot of money before that.

I believed everything my brother, Albert told me and he used my gullability to his advantage. He made me interested in what he wanted me to do, by telling me what he called a "vital secret," which only he knew about. He said that his vital secret was connected to a potential threat to the safety of the western world. "I'll tell you," he said, "You're not to repeat it. Only you and I will know about it. I've got a strong influence over most heads of state and I advise them regularly on the phone."

"I believed him, even though he was only eleven years old.

"Well, what's your secret?" I asked him.

Albert spoke in a hushed tone of voice. "I'm bribing Khrushchev[11*] with seven shillings and six pence a week not to drop a hydrogen bomb on London. "If I don't pay him, he will do so."

"How long have you been paying him?" I asked.

"Since the Cuban Crisis."

"What's the Cuban Crisis?"

"Nothing you need worry your pretty little head about. Khrushchev is a fucking dangerous man."

"You said a naughty word just then. I'll tell Daddy."

"Never mind that. Khrushchev has told me that my act of paying him deserves a reward and that he will launch his missiles within one hour if he is not rewarded."

"How will you reward him?" I asked.

"Ah-ha! That's where we come to the point," said Albert. He continued, "He feels most strongly that you should run errands for me, whenever I ask you to, generally fetch and carry for me, make my bed, cover my toothbrush with toothpaste and make a bolt for it whenever I shout 'errand'!"

I was completely taken in. "How will Khrushchev find out if I refuse to do what you want?" I asked.

"Very easily," replied Albert. "Do you remember when some men came to the house last week, dressed up as workmen?"

"Yes. What about them?"

"They weren't really workmen. They were Soviet or Russian agents disguised as workmen. They were sent by the Russian government to bug the house, that is to say, to put wires and microphones behind the walls of every room. That was to make sure that you run errands for me, whenever I want you to. That way, Khrushchev will know immediately if you refuse to run errands for me, and his first reaction will be to nuke London."

11 *Nikita Khrushchev – Former President of the USSR. He was almost guilty of annihilating the western world, during the Cuban Crisis.

"Is this really true?"

"I'm afraid it is. Every word of it."

"All right, I'll do everything you tell me to do."

"That's my boy!"

I ran errands for Albert for about a month. I even did up his shoe laces. Eventually, I became suspicious.

"How do you manage to get the seven shillings and six pence a week posted to Khrushchev?" I asked.

"That's easy. I just write him a cheque for seven shillings and six pence. Then I put it into an envelope marked 'Urgent Life-Saving Powders', and I address the envelope to Comrade Nikita Khrushchev, c/o The Kremlin, Moscow, USSR."

"May I post these letters for you myself?" I asked.

"Oh, no, Khrushchev says I've got to do that, without anyone seeing me doing it."

I finally realized that I had been taken for a ride.

Albert and I were sitting in the garden at our house in Berkshire, some months after the Cuban Crisis.

Albert said, "Go up to my bedroom and bring me a book called, *Lady Chatterley's Lover*? It's onmy bedside table."

"No, I don't think I will," I replied.

"Have you no compassion for us poor, poor Londoners?" said Albert.

The Professor finished typing and straightened his tie. "That story's not sick like many of Charlie's stories," he said, adding, "It shows him to be absolutely half-witted, even for a six-year-old. No wonder he was so retarded when he became an adult."

Esmerelda's eyes filled with tears, which trickled down her cheeks. "You haven't got a single kind word to say about Charlie," she said. *"He was my friend, faithful and just to me."* Julius Caesar. Act 2, Scene 1."

"It's actually Act 3, Scene 2, corrected the Professor with a sneer.

Another of Charlie's Stories

Mayhem on the Eight Fifteen

Albert was fifteen years old and I was ten years old. We were travelling on a train from Reading to Paddington, London.

"We want the whole compartment to ourselves and that means ourselves," Albert said to me assertively. "I'm going to lie down on the luggage rack, and I'm going to read aloud '*The Fall of the House of Usher*' by Edgar Allan Poe, in a loud, menacing monotone, and you are going to sing, '*Everything's up to date in Kansas City,*' equally as loudly.

Unfortunately, a passenger sent for the guard who complained to my father. Albert was made to learn the first fifteen verses of *Horatius,* and I was sent to bed without any dinner. Fortunately, Albert loves *Horatius* and I took pleasure in going to bed without any dinner, because I had had three boxes of *brie* the night before which made me feel sick.

My father said something very amusing to Albert about his performance on the train, "A boy who lies down on the luggage rack of a train, reading aloud, '*The Fall of the House of Usher*' in a loud, menacing monotone is *mentally* ill."

"I agree wholeheartedly with that remark," said the Professor. "It's a pity Charlie failed to inherit his wise father's genes."

Another of Charlie's Stories

When I Jumped Onto My
Head Teacher's Back

The head teacher of Eddistone's, my junior school, was called Cameron Buckner. Buckner had a murderous temper, looked just like Abraham Lincoln, and walked about followed by a grossly over-weight black sausage dog, with the extraordinary name of Blockbuster, which permanently sniffed at his heels.

I was eleven years old when I took my eleven plus.

When Buckner told me that I had passed the exam, I was so carried away with euphoria, that I jumped onto his back, bringing him to the floor. He was sixty five years old and wasn't all that fit. He took quite a few minutes to get to his feet, while his fat, black sausage dog sniffed anxiously round his supine body.

It would be an understatement to say that Buckner was not very pleased with me on that occasion.

"I'm sorry to have to criticize your friend, Charlie all the time, but on this occasion, like on other occasions, he comes over as being a pathetic delinquent," said the Professor.

Another of Charlie's Stories

The Kinky NatWest Bank Manager

I read English at university. When I was a student, I did a clerical job in a NatWest bank but the libel laws prevent me from naming its location or indeed its manager.

It did not take me long to find out that the bank manager was a real Queen Mary, as Guy Burgess would have put it. He was also a sex pervert. His name was Bobby Phillips (not his real name).

One morning, Phillips summoned me to his office. He was standing up. He was short and bald and spoke with a London accent. He was holding up a pair of pink lady's knickers which were edged with lace.

"You sent for me, sir?" I said, struggling to keep a straight face.

"Yes. I want your opinion."

"About what, sir? I asked.

"If I were to put these knickers on, do you think I would fill them out nicely?"

"What with, sir?" I replied.

It appeared that my words had upset him. He gave me a defeated look and said, "That will be all, except that I've got a tape here for you to give to Debbie Page. I want her to type all of it. One top and two carbons, please; one copy is to go in the clients' file in alphabetical order and the second copy is to go to my office."

"All right. I will do that, sir," I said.

* * *

"'Are you Debbie Page?'" I asked.

"Yes, what if I am?"

"Debbie, Mr Phillips would like you to type this tape. He wants one top and two carbons." I repeated the rest of Phillips's instructions. Debbie had short peroxide hair, a fringe and disfiguring acne.

She snatched the tape from my hand.

"Why me?" she asked rudely.

"Those are Mr Phillips's orders," I said coldly. I didn't want to get involved in other people's rows at the workplace."

Debbie crossed her legs and fed the tape into her machine. She began to type. On one side of the tape were letters to people with overdrafts, all except for a ribald limerick at the end.

A colonel there was from Belgrade,

Who found a dead whore in a cave.

He must have had pluck, to have had a cold fuck,

But think of the money he saved.

"Debbie stormed over to where I was sitting. She blamed me for having given her the tape.

"My function at this bank is to obey Mr Phillips's orders, not to question them," I said. She sneered at me. She never spoke to me again.

As for the kinky bank manager, I dined out about him all over London. Eventually, he got into *Private Eye*.

The Professor took off his jacket and sighed.

"I don't understand what Charlie meant by saying that the

bank manager was a ‘real Queen Mary – as Guy Burgess would have put it’. What on earth did he mean? There’s no evidence in the story to suggest that he was gay, only that he was kinky.

“Incidentally, I loathe this story. It’s really sick, like most of Charlie’s stories. I simply don’t understand the nature of your extraordinary friendship with him.”

Another of Charlie's Stories

The Debauched Psychiatrist
Laugh Not, Little Brother When a Hearse Goes By

I was sent to a Harley Street psychiatrist once, because of my fascination for the macabre. His name was Morgan Whitteradged. I was about fifteen years old at the time. Incidentally, he was absolutely bonkers.

He always wore riding breeches, riding boots and a bright red hunting jacket.

In order to put his patients at their case, he swaggered into his consulting room, slapped his thigh with his riding crop and said the following:

"Absolutely strapping stuff, sex, hey what! Do you want to hear what I do just afterwards? I bung my stinking carcass out of bed, wipe the spunk off my Hampton, crash into a bath and go for a spiffing good run round the block. Then I bugger up to the kitchen, where I make four socking good crumpets, all of them absolutely s-q-u-e-l-c-h-i-n-g with butter. After I've eaten them, I bowl upstairs to the bedroom and I start all over again, what!

"By the way, what do you think of Dostoevsky? Dashed depressing writer, what!"

"I like his works," I replied.

"Oh, you do, do you? What's your problem, young man?

What are your hobbies, when you're not reading fucking Dostoevsky? What turns you on?"

"I like going to funerals. I get sexual pleasure out of seeing coffins being lowered into graves. I love bloodthirsty things in general. In particular, I like witnessing operations and watching post-mortems."

There was a pause.

"I really ought to admit you to a clinic," said Whitteradge. He picked up his phone and started to make a call.

At that moment, I was terrified. I propelled myself through the window of his Harley Street consulting room, breaking the glass, and ran as fast and as far as I possibly could. I ran all the way from Harley Street to our house in Kensington. I didn't stop running until I got home. Then I locked the front door and bolted it behind me."

"No comment," said the acid-tongued Professor.

Another of Charlie's Stories

Calling the Samaritans

I have never been averse to smut or indeed to black humour.

I was writing a really black humoured book during one of my university vacations. I write my books at night and sometimes do temporary jobs during the day. I drink a lot of coffee to give myself the energy to work.

After working for some hours, I wanted to print what I had written. Try as I did, I couldn't get my toner into my printer. It was then four o'clock in the morning. My hands and arms were covered with ink which really distressed me.

Finally, I decided to call the Samaritans, whose lines were engaged for over an hour. A man answered eventually. "I'm very upset indeed," I said. "I'm writing a book and I can't get my toner to go into my printer, which means that I can't print my work. Could you send a man out to help me, please. Do you realize that my hands and arms are covered with ink?"

The man was overtly rude and un-cooperative. He said, "The Samaritans cater for psychologically distressed people, not for those who are unable to use the tools of their trade. Do you think a dentist would ring us up and ask us to fit a burr to his drill?"

"What the hell's a burr?" I asked.

The disagreeable man hung up.

The Professor wiped his forehead with the back of his hand. "I don't find that story at all funny," he said. "Your friend, Charlie is what they call a professional clown whom no one should take seriously." He added, "I'm so relieved that he refrains from describing the book he had written."

Another of Charlie's Stories

The Tradesman's Entrance

I heard about an unspeakable gynaecologist, called Frank Denny. He was a Harley boy. I am friendly with the woman who had been consulting him. She said that he was incompetent, coarse, clumsy, insolent, arrogant and sadistic. She added that each of this cacophony of adjectives applied to him. He spoke with a heavy Glaswegian accent. He gave her the following advice:-

"If your front entrance is indisposed, you need feel no qualms about using the tradesmen's entrance, but would you be sure to grease your partner's member if you've just passed a motion."

My friend reported this patron saint of sodomy to the General Medical Council but predictably, they did sweet F.A."

"That's another ghastly story, but I'm obliged to listen to you telling me all Charlie's stories, because I'm being paid to do so," said the Professor.

Esmerelda delighted in accounting for the stories which Charlie told. It gave her sexual pleasure to shock and disgust the Professor.

Another of Charlie's Stories

The Prostitute, the X-Rays and the Catherine Wheel

I was hurrying in London's West End, trying to buy a theatre ticket. I wanted to see *Stephen Ward*. I fell over and sprained my ankle. I had to go to hospital for x-rays and bandages. I shelved the idea of buying a theatre ticket. I wanted to go home. It was raining and I couldn't get a taxi.

I noticed a sign saying *Minicabs*. I went into the building and up a staircase. The first door I came to was on the third floor. I assumed that it led to an office from which minicabs could be hired. I heard movements on the other side of the door. I knocked several times but was ignored.

My foot was hurting a lot by this time and my patience had run out. I took a few steps backwards, ran forwards towards the door and threw my weight against it.

The door gave way. Its hinges were ripped off. It was an exceptionally thin door, like a sheet of cardboard. It smashed to the floor of the room, causing a cloud of dust to rise into the air, floating like snowflakes.

I over-balanced and tumbled into the room. My x-rays were scattered over the floor.

A bright silk screen was facing me. From behind it, rushed an astounded prostitute in the livery of her trade. She was wearing fish-net stockings, a corset and she was carrying a whip. My foot was hurting so much that I lost my temper.

"If this is a disorderly house, why the hell isn't there a sign outside, saying that it's a fucking disorderly house?" I demanded.

"Sod off!" shouted the prostitute.

"I'm trying to get a taxi. Have you got any idea how much pain I'm in? Do you realize that my foot is done up in bandages?"

"It's not my frigging business," shouted the prostitute.

"You don't believe me, do you? Why don't you take a look at these x-rays?" I asked nonsensically.

An unhealthy-looking, grey-skinned punter, wearing only an off-white T-shirt, ambled from behind the screen and shouted furiously at the prostitute.

"What's up, woman? I've just paid you thirty bloody quid. I'm not nearly ready to come yet. I want my thirty quid back."

The prostitute screwed the banknotes into a ball, and threw them into the punter's face.

"Here's what you can do with your fucking money!" she bellowed.

I left the building as quickly as I could. I was ashamed of having caused the prostitute's door to come off its hinges, jeopardizing her safety and depriving her of thirty pounds.

I went to a pub, ordered a gin and tonic and some peanuts, and thought about a way of repaying the prostitute for the damage that I'd done to her property.

In an hour's time, I dragged myself upstairs to her room once more. The broken door was leaning against the inside wall. I could hear movements and sounds suggestive of sexual activity.

"Er, hullo, there!" I ventured.

The prostitute stormed up to me in a violent rage. She was naked. I said,

"First, let me say how dreadfully sorry I am, to have

interrupted you a second time when you were in the course of your er… unconventional but courageous business. I want to talk to you about your door."

"If you don't fuck off, I'll jab you with a used heroin needle! I've got AIDS."

I was terrified. "Don't do that!" I shouted. I added, "I've just come to tell you that I know a man who can put some new hinges onto your door. When would it be convenient for him to do this? Perhaps, you could get your diary out and we could arrange a date."

The pattern of events was the same. Another livid punter, this time, a muscular black man, came out from behind the screen, naked like the prostitute.

"Hey, fella, back off, will ya!"

The prostitute advanced towards me, her eyes demonic. She was brandishing a syringe with a residue of blood in it. The punter gaped at me with raven's eyes.

I threw the x-rays at the prostitute in blind terror and rushed out into the corridor. I curled myself into a ball (God knows how) and rolled downstairs into the street like a Catherine wheel.

"This doesn't seem to be my lucky day," I muttered to myself.

"That's one of Charlie's typically sordid stories," said the Professor, adding, "Is it autobiographical by any chance?"

"Yes, you bet it is," lied Esmerelda arrogantly, "I aim to shock."

"Well, I don't aim to be shocked," said the Professor. "I aim to be enlightened."

"Those are all the Charlie stories which I've got to tell you," said Esmerelda. "Now, I'm going to talk to you about my own experiences, and you're going to listen to me, whether you like it or not."

"I suppose I haven't got much choice," said the Professor coldly. "I do hope this isn't going to take too long."

The Patient Speaks

These were the stories which Charlie Yates told to his audiences. I had been in Marseille for a while. When I came back to London, there was no sign of Charlie among my friends.

"I asked Trout where he was. Trout said that he had been suffering from terrible headaches, that he had been staying with his mother, and that he had been told by his doctor to go to bed at six o'clock every evening.

"We all missed him dreadfully, but somehow we managed to get on with our lives.

"During Charlie's absence, I spent my days in London, between ten thirty and noon, attending post-mortems at Bede's Hospital which Charlie had also visited.

"My friend, Annabella Sikes also had a fascination for the macabre. Like myself, she was a close friend of Charlie's. We were both out of work.

"Annabella was taller than me. She had long black hair, which was swept back from her face in a ponytail and secured by an ivory slide. She had a pale, unblemished skin and large green eyes. She spoke with a slightly Canadian accent.

"Her previous job had been to take down minutes of a company meeting. Her company director had told her to do something about her written style. She paid no attention to him, however, and regarded her written style as being a stamp of her individuality.

"To give some idea of her inappropriate style of minute-taking, this is an example of the way she described the opening of one meeting.

'"Chairman Jones was grimy and unshaven. He was wearing an ill-fitting, dirt-stained shirt and soiled blue jeans. He kicked open the door and lurched towards the conference table, chewing a three-day-old cigar butt which he spat on to the floor. He might just as well have walked straight out of a street brawl. With an effort, he forced his mouth to form a grimace as close to a smile as he could. He had teeth like piano keys and stank like a badger. He exhaled the stench of stale whisky.

'"His eyes swollen and bloodshot after about ten days' heavy boozing, he eyed his colleagues menacingly, loosened his tie, hiccoughed and emptied the contents of a filthy old carrier bag onto the conference table.

'"Been fiddlin' the accounts again, Palsy?" he snarled at the company treasurer as he dug him sharply in the ribs.

"The treasurer's heart skipped a beat. He was a slightly built, well-groomed guy, wearing a dark pin-striped suit and a red carnation. He blushed profusely and hurriedly left the room to call his bookkeeper."

"Annabella was definitely in the wrong. Chairman Jones, although slovenly in his appearance, was apparently a teetotaller who sang in his church choir and who was highly respectable.

"The company director took a grim view of Annabella's prose. '"Are you an authority on cardiology, Miss Sikes?"' he asked her, after summoning her into his office.

"No, sir."

"How in the world can you tell whether or not the heart of a man sitting some feet away from you, is skipping a beat?"

"Poetic licence, dear boy."

"Don't you dare address me as 'dear boy'. You will call me

'sir'," the director bawled. "Besides these are supposed to be the minutes of a meeting, not a novel by James Hadley Chase!"

"Annabella went on arguing and accusing her adversary of outmoded pomposity, which, she said, had left the country at the same time as the penny-farthing. She was fired instantly.

"As Annabella and I were both out of work, we attended post-mortems at Bede's Hospital. We were admitted to the post-mortem room by the eccentric Gomer Evans, not long after his identical twin brother, Leslie, had met his untimely death. Both brothers were dwarves and had pronounced O.C.D.[12*] Leslie was the dwarf who had pestered Charlie incessantly on the phone.

"Annabella and I paid him ten pounds each to let us into the post-mortem room. He also gave us white coats, which had been stolen from a locker room and which it was compulsory to wear at post-mortems.

"Gomer Evans's entire conversation, delivered in a hypermanic monologue, revolved round letters which he had written to the Mayor of Londonderry, asking him for permission to participate in the Orangemen's marches during the four weeks' holiday that he took every year.

"Neither Annabella nor I were interested in any of this talk. We were only interested in using him as a lever to get us into the post-mortem room when it was being used.

"The post-mortem room at Bede's is not very big. The person lecturing the medical students was an eminent and brilliant man called Dr Spearpoint, whose manner corresponded aptly with his name. He was of medium height, had white, swept-back hair and staring blue eyes. He was about fifty years old. He swore robustly enough to make a fishwife blush, when he was irritated. He was also known to have a tongue like a viper. When he questioned any luckless student, whose attention he thought was wandering, he did not need a scalpel to cut the student's throat with. His tongue was sharper than a scalpel.

12 *O.C.D.: Obsessive compulsive disorder

"Some medical students were terrified of speaking to him during post-mortems. They didn't dare to show their ignorance. It was common practice for a more retiring student to take refuge behind a fellow student's shoulder when Spearpoint looked in his direction.

"I talked to one student called Rupert Peacock who looked pretty timid. Annabella thought that he was as wet as a melon. He told us that he had been so frightened of asking questions during post-mortems, that he had tried to break the ice, by talking to Spearpoint about a neutral subject outside the post-mortem room. Peacock followed Spearpoint to the hospital car park. Spearpoint got into his car and lowered his window, "Yes, Peacock, what do you want?" he asked impatiently.

"Excuse me, sir," Peacock ventured in a faltering tone of voice, "I do so like your Ford."

"It's not a Ford," replied Spearpoint, revving up the engine, "It's a fucking Ferrari!"

"Spearpoint had a very black sense of humour. Although a lot of his medical jokes were too technical for Annabella and me to understand, his audiences seemed to find them witty. Some students cackled loudly; others merely chuckled.

"The practice of conducting a post-mortem was routine, and, even to those with no medical knowledge, was straightforward. Spearpoint insisted that the organs of the deceased should be examined before the bodies were brought into the room. At each post-mortem, Evans, the dwarf, brought in a metal tray, carrying the organs removed from the bodies, and laid the tray in front of Spearpoint, like a butler serving a tray of dinner to an aristocrat. After the dissection and examination of each organ, Spearpoint told Evans to wheel in the butchered body, to which these organs had belonged.

"Spearpoint never gave the names of the deceased. First, he gave the person's age and briefly stated what his or her personal habits were (only if they were related to the person's death). Finally, he stated the circumstances in which loss of life had taken place.

"This lung that I am holding," Spearpoint began, "belonged to an eighty-eight-year-old man who had smoked over sixty cigarettes a day, for at least seventy years of his life. Can we be at all surprised, therefore, that he suffered from terminal carcinoma of the lung? See here," he said, as he held the allegedly diseased lung upwards towards the light, "Here we shall find the carcinoma. It stands out like a sort thumb, if you'll excuse the cliché."

"Spearpoint continued to look at the lung as if it were an address book without the address he wanted in it, and suddenly blushed profusely.

"Can't find it, blast it!" he exclaimed aggressively. He looked questioningly at Evans who was standing about five feet away from him. He whispered something to the unfortunate dwarf, whose responsibility it had been to hand him the right material. The dwarf said something to Spearpoint and looked humiliated.

"That's the wrong lung, you fucking fool!" Spearpoint shouted. His words were heard by the medical students who sniggered into their hands.

"I'm only doing my best," said the dwarf.

"I don't want to hear about your blasted, bloody best!" Spearpoint shouted, "When, clearly your best is not good enough." He shook the healthy lung in the air like a dish cloth, and threw it into the dwarf's face. He picked up the other lung on the tray, and handed a repulsive-looking object back to Spearpoint.

"Et voila!" Spearpoint beamed, searching for admiration on the students' faces, "the carcinoma stands out half a mile."

"Spearpoint made a brief examination of the other organs extracted from the body of the eighty-eight-year-old man. He found nothing untoward about any of them, other than the wear of old age. He diagnosed carcinoma of the lung as being the cause of the man's death.

"All right, you can take the tray away now, Evans," he said peremptorily.

"*Mister* Evans to you!" the dwarf retorted.

"Why, of course, *Mister* Evans," Spearpoint said, using the word 'Mister' sarcastically. He could not afford to omit the word when its use had been requested in the past. This was because of his fear of repercussions from NUPE of which Evans was an active and militant member. Spearpoint remembered the previous occasion, when there had been a strike by workers in the post-mortem room; even the freezers had been out of action. He turned green.

"Would you please be so kind, Mr Evans, he said, with artificial courtesy, quite alien to his nature, "and fetch the eighty-eight-year-old's body from the freezer."

"During the five minute interim period, between the time Evans went outside to locate the body in the freezer, and the time he swiftly wheeled it into the post-mortem room, everybody could hear him singing at the top of his voice. He was singing a very well-known Irish song, which went like this:

"As I came home on a Monday night, as drunk as drunk could be"

...(the sound of someone wrenching open a heavy door)...

"I saw a horse outside the door where my own horse should be"

...(a clanking sound of the heavy door being slammed shut, followed by the thudding sound of something being thrown onto an object propelled by wheels, and the sound of something hollow like a head hitting something made of metal, followed by the sound of Evans muttering the word "fuck" at the top of his voice)

"And I called my wife and I said to her, would you kindly tell to me..."

"Can we please be doing without that disgusting word?" said Spearpoint loudly enough for Evans to hear him. Evans continued to sing.

"Who owns that horse outside the door where my own horse should be?

" 'You're drunk, you're drunk, you silly old fool, and still you cannot see,

That's a loverly sow that my mother sent to me' —

"Well it's many a day I've travelled, a hundred miles or more,

"But a saddle on a sow, sure I never did see before!"

"Oh, I do wish you'd stop that singing, Mr Evans," Spearpoint complained as the dwarf wheeled in the deceased. "This is a post-mortem room, not a public house on a Saturday night, and I can hardly hear myself speak!"

"The eighty-eight-year-old deceased's body was not a pretty sight. It might just as well have been slung onto a hook in a butcher's shop. The body was yellowish and rubbery. What dignity it had had in life, had been hacked away. Its eyes had not even been closed, and its mouth was frozen in a hideous grimace.

"Well, there's old Smokey for you," said Spearpoint. "Ever heard the song 'On Top of Old Smokey'? Well, this disease seems to have made the grade now, what! Please note," he continued, "Even the teeth, or what is left of them, are the colour of mahogany. That's what nicotine does to you.

He continued, "All right, Mr Evans, you can sling the meat back to the freezer, now. Serves the fucker right." He then cracked a medical joke which neither Annabella nor I could understand. The joke caused the medical students to laugh sycophantically.

"Annabella and I were amused by a wordy notice in black Victorian letters, on the wall of the post-mortem room. The notice read as follows:

"Drinking in the post-mortem room is permitted in view of the sometimes harrowing nature of the proceedings witnessed. Actual drunkenness, however, is strictly forbidden, and anyone found guilty of such an offence, will be banned from entering the post-mortem room for three months.

"I had noticed that some medical students were drinking but were still sober. Annabella and I had a bottle of gin between us, but we didn't drink much because we hadn't read the notice. We soon found out that some medical students had been knocking back booze like lemonade.

* * *

Evans had predicted that the last post-mortem that morning was going to be much more interesting and unusual than the first post-mortem.

"We're having a brain tumour today," he said, rubbing his hands like a child announcing the arrival of his favourite pudding. He smiled as he took our ten-pound notes to let us through the door. However, he added gleefully that he was raising the price to twenty pounds due to the brain tumour.

"There's only one more piece of meat to come," he stated. He added, "Brain tumours are not all that common. This time it's a young 'un, a man somewhere in his twenties, which is even more rare."

"Annabella and I wondered whether or not the man had been good-looking. We agreed that it was a pity that Charlie wasn't there. We knew that he would have dined out on the exhibit all over London. He would have made it into a joke, to hide his misery and disgust, due to the fact that a man should die so young.

"The next exhibit followed the same procedure as before. Evans came into the room, carrying the metal tray, bearing the heart, two clean-looking lungs, a liver, a couple of kidneys, a bladder, a brain – correct me if I've left anything out. I don't think I have – and handed the tray to Spearpoint.

"This is a most unusual case," said Spearpoint, pointing with a cane to some skull X-rays taken at different angles. They had been clipped on to an illuminated screen, high up on the wall. Annabella and I were in the front row of the gallery, and were taking it in turns to look through a pair of opera glasses which I had stolen from a theatre.

"This patient, a man in his late twenties, early thirties, had been complaining of what he described as 'agonizing' headaches for about a month. They got progressively worse," Spearpoint explained, "The man went to his GP who arranged for some X-rays to be taken of his skull. As you can all see from the X-rays, absolutely no abnormality was detected. A report was sent back to the man's GP who said the pains were psychological.

"Finally, after three weeks, the patient went back to his GP, and complained of 'horrendous' headaches which he said were getting worse. His GP sent him to a specialist and he was given a CT scan of the brain.

"According to the CT scan, which I am pointing at, there was definitely a tumour. This was pear-shaped and was twice the size of a walnut. It had formed itself above the cerebellum of the brain. The tumour shown on the CT scan was so far up in the brain, that it would not have been possible to operate on it. It was simply a question of a few weeks before the patient was clinically dead."

"On the CT scan shown to the medical students, there was a mass of something, but without medical knowledge, it was impossible to say what this represented. Spearpoint went on to talk about this unfortunate man's brain, in language that was totally incomprehensible to us. After cutting the brain in half like a piece of cheese and extracting the tumour, Spearpoint told the medical students that the tumour was malignant. He took it off the tray and put it onto a smaller tray to be passed from one medical student to another. He asked each student to comment on the consistency of the tumour.

"One of the people he chose was Annabella, who had to hold the tray bearing the tumour. She didn't know what to say, so she pointed to her throat, whispering the words, "Laryngitis; can't speak." I had to make a great effort not to laugh but I'm afraid Spearpoint noticed my amusement:

"Perhaps your friend, who is so amused by your disability, would care to throw some light on the consistency of this tumour?" he said pompously.

"I put on a thick German accent and used broken English. I said that following my training at a medical college in Berlin, I thought that the thing was more likely to be a multiple clot than a tumour.

"Tain't so, sa!" a man, who had obviously been reading the Flashman books, shouted from the back row, and he, like Spearpoint, began to use technical jargon beyond our comprehension. The man was exceptionally tall and abnormally thin, and had frizzy, gypsy-like black hair. Overall, he looked like a freak.

"Carcinoma is a disease, hitherto unconquered by the Medical Profession," shouted Spearpoint manically. He continued, "Mankind has not as yet discovered how to cure it. Mankind has not even managed to find out what causes it, where it comes from…" Spearpoint was interrupted by the freak.

"I know; I can tell you! It comes from nuclear waste and it's the Russians who started the disease." The freak's voice rose to a startling crescendo. He thought that Spearpoint was ludicrous and lacking in judgement.

"I'll tell you where the disease comes from," added the freak. "It sings to us from the Steppes, do you hear? It sings to us all the way from the Steppes, like the voice of Tolstoy!"

"For Christ's sake, get this maniac out of here, Evans. Oh, I mean, Mr Evans," Spearpoint said irritably. The freak resisted being forcibly moved, but Evans was remarkably strong and deftly carried him out of the post-mortem room, using a firemans lift.

"This incident interrupted the post-mortem for at least five minutes. The medical students were convulsed with laughter. Even Spearpoint had to make an effort to keep a straight face.

"All right, Mr Evans," he said, after composing himself, "Time's getting short. Put the tumour and the brain back onto the main tray with all the other – I don't hasten to add – healthy organs, and go out and get the meat. Please be quick, I'm supposed to be lunching with the Minister of Health, blast it!"

"I could see that Evans was in an euphoric mood. This was due to the manner in which he had disposed of the freak. Also, he had extracted plenty of money from Annabella and me. In addition, he was drunk. He also knew that whatever misdemeanour he committed (provided it wasn't cannibalism or necrophilia) he could not possibly lose his job since the loss of his job would cause NUPE to bring Bede's to a standstill.

"Once he found out that Spearpoint's schedule had fallen behind, Evans skuttled out of the room like someone trying to catch a train. While he was outside, looking for the deceased, he started to sing loudly and drunkenly. The medical students couldn't hear Spearpoint speak. All they could hear was the rendering of part of a very well- known song:

"There rises a tomb where the blue Danube flows,

Engraved there in characters clear,

Oh, stranger when passing, oh pray for the soul Of Abdul Abulbul Amir. "

"Spearpoint made an effort to keep his temper, but because of the shortness of Evans's outrageous outburst, he decided to let it ride. He raised his voice and told his students the difference between X-rays and CT scans. By the time Evans had entered the post-mortem room wheeling the young deceased, his mood, unlike that of Spearpoint, was ecstatic. He rolled in the trolley at a run, like someone about to mount a bicycle going downhill. For a moment, I thought he was going to swing his weight onto the trolley.

“‘*Clang, clang, clang, went the trolley!*’ he sang briefly. *“Ring, ring, ring, went the bell.”* He continued to run alongside the trolley, as he pushed it towards his astounded onlookers. It occurred to me that he had been taking drugs, and that he was dependent on our donations to finance them. While propelling the trolley towards the centre of the post-mortem room, he began to sing yet another song, slightly longer this time. There was a glazed expression in his eyes, and the song went like this:

“So what care I for my house and land,
What need have I of my treasure-o
What need have I of my newly wedded lord,
When I can go off with the gypsies o”

“For Christ’s sake, shut up, Evans!” screamed Spearpoint at the top of his voice, “I will not tolerate this perpetual singing! Why do you do this to me?” He went on, and surprised us all by a sudden display of emotion, coming from a man of such apparently inhuman calm. “What in the world have you got against me, Mr Evans? You are turning me into a nervous wreck. Every night, just as I am about to go to sleep, a bus passes my house and changes gear. I wake up in a cold sweat, shouting: ‘My God, Evans is singing outside my house. He knows where I live. He has come to torment me and deprive me of my sleep.”

“I am a Welshman!” said Evans indignantly. “How dare you compare my singing with the sound of a bus changing gear!”

“I could compare it with many other things, far worse than that,” said Spearpoint, “but I don’t propose to interrupt this post-mortem any further by listing them. When I tell you repeatedly that your singing disturbs my post-mortems, why do you go on doing it?” He was almost in tears.

"Evans was taken aback by Spearpoint's display of emotion. He quietly resumed his duties, showing respect towards his boss.

"Annabella and I were both paralytically drunk, so we missed seeing the deceased's face.

"Give me those," said Annabella, trying to take the opera glasses from my hand, "I want to see the stiff!" Her speech was markedly slurred.

"You'll see it in your own good time. Lack not the virtue of patience," I said in a tone of voice designed to annoy. "I stole them, not you, so I'll have the first view." I was only aware when I'd said this, that my words rhymed.

"I picked up the bottle of gin from the floor and drank from it. With my other hand I focused the opera glasses onto the body of the deceased, butchered from one end to the other, like all the other bodies. Evans was standing between the head and my line of vision, so I couldn't see the face.

"Oh I do so wish that silly little man would get out of the way!" I said, "Anyone would think we weren't paying him to let us in here."

"Evans stepped aside and finally enabled me to focus the opera glasses on the face of the deceased. It was two feet away from Annabella and me. What I saw was horrible. It is hard to say what happens to the mind after a major shock. I received a message which was designed to batter my body first and my mind later. I felt as if my head had been soaked in a bucket of iced water. The numbness I felt radiated from my ears to my jaw, until it reached every tooth in my head. Then it radiated to my shoulders and arms. I could hear the childlike urgency in Annabella's voice, as she kept repeating the words, "Give me those! Give me those!" She had not yet seen the deceased's face.

"I could no longer hold the opera glasses and I dropped them. I walked away from Annabella.

"She asked me where I was going. She had not been given a chance to look at the face of the deceased.

"I went on walking, until I came to the slab on which the deceased lay. I looked at the label on one of the toes. It was confirmed whose body lay on the slab. I remembered the familiar words: "He's had such bad headaches lately".

"I knew what Annabella and I had paid twenty pounds to see, and all I was aware of was the acute pain which had descended from my shoulders to the hands.

"I looked closely at the deceased. A deep cut had been made from the pelvic region to the neck. The flesh had been prized apart like the division of the Red Sea, and secured at either side of the body by metal clamps. It was hollow inside. What had been removed was on the metal tray which we had been ogling.

"The head had been shaved. The top of the head had been lopped off like an egg. There was nothing where the brain had been. A few remaining wisps of hair, which had not been shaved off, were covered with blood. The only good thing which I can say about what I saw, was that the mouth was in repose, and not in the hideous grimace that I had seen on the faces of the other bodies.

"I screamed at intermittent intervals, and during the interludes between the screaming, I heard Spearpoint's voice: "What the dickens is going on in here?" "Dash it all, Evans, you were supposed to check everybody at the door."

"Evans didn't answer, and walked nervously up and down with the tray bearing the organs in one hand, and a hatchet, with which he had cut off the top of the head, in the other. He sauntered towards me as Spearpoint tried to get his attention once more.

"Do put those bloody things down, Evans," he boomed peremptorily, "They're not canapés at a cocktail party!"

"Evans put the hatchet down. He left it lying blade upwards

between the grids on the drain underneath the deceased. He dropped the tray so clumsily that the brain fell off the tray onto the floor. I went on screaming until I fainted, but I was only unconscious for a few seconds. I woke up finding the brain impaled on my stiletto heel. I noticed from the markings on the floor, that it had slithered about a foot away from where Evans had dropped it. When I turned my head, I found that the upturned hatchet was about a foot away from my skull. If it had been a quarter of an inch closer, it would have cut straight through my skull and killed me outright.

"Well well well!" said Evans, as he leaned over me, blowing the smell of stale beer into my face, "Your life was saved by his brain."

"This same skull was Yorick's skull, the King's Jester…

"A fellow of infinite jest, of most excellent fancy, "

Hamlet Act V, Scene 1

"I recited these words, partly to myself and partly out loud, instinctively remembering the lines from *Hamlet* which I had been made to learn by heart as a child, as a punishment for throwing a brick at a passing Rolls Royce,

I also remembered the remainder of the lines,

"He hath borne me on his back a thousand times,; and now how, abhorred in my imagination it is."

"Whoever he was, your life was saved by his brain," said Evans .He started to laugh unhealthily. I recalled the occasion when I had heard these words before, and started screaming again, until an invisible hand felt its way into my head, and turned me off at the mains," said Esmerelda, having spoken at considerable length.

"That's all I've got to tell you, Professor," said Esmerelda, having spoken at considerable length.

"As for my friend, Annabella Sikes, she went home and hanged herself. She was my best friend so her death hurt me almost as much as Charlie's."

"I can't comment on your ghoulish adventures, Esmerelda," said the Professor disapprovingly, "other than to say, you're a morbid little brat. You deserved everything you got. Apart from that, you've wasted hours of my valuable time. I don't know which of you I hate most, you or your despicable friend, Charlie."

"I've had enough of your disgusting insults, Stone!" shouted Esmerelda, showing rage for the first time since the interviews had started. She added, "Fuck off, you obnoxious, repulsive Yank!"

The Failure of the Mission of Professor Stone

Professor Isaac Stone had typed every word uttered by Esmerelda Harris, during his two hourly interviews with her, each interview ending with severe withdrawal symptoms, so odious to watch that he had to wait in the corridor while the orderlies held her down. In his report, he did not refer to the interruptions. He typed Esmerelda's story as if it had been a monologue, lasting for up to twenty-four hours.

Esmerelda went to the mirror and found that her face had not aged, in spite of the drugs with which she had been injected, for an unknown amount of time, perhaps days, perhaps weeks.

She swept back her reddish blonde hair, and secured it with two gold combs. She put on a pair of white velvet trousers and a matching white cashmere sweater. Over the white trousers she pulled on a pair of wine-red boots. Round her neck, she placed a gold pendant bearing the words:

In the event of death, cremate my body. Scatter my ashes over Marseille harbour.

She hoped that her suicide would serve as a form of revenge against the Professor, and his systematic cruelty towards her.

She put gold earrings onto each ear, and a little blue dust under her eyes to match her irises.

She went to the window and noticed that the ground was

white. She estimated that the month was either January or February.

She looked out of the window, and saw St Paul's Cathedral for the last time. She climbed out of the window and sat on the snowy ledge. Eventually, she slid off it and as the ground came towards her, she smiled.

In loving memory of Charles Edward Yates, our dearly loved court-jester who died prematurely.